This book is dedicated to all the
donor families who have chosen
to give the ultimate gift.
The gift of life.

CHAPTER ONE

SARAH HENDERSON STUDIED the computer chart in front of her. She didn't like the way ten-year-old Lindsey's lab work was trending. With the child already in heart failure, what had started out as a cold had quickly turned into a respiratory infection. Now even with intravenous antibiotic treatment she seemed to be deteriorating daily.

"There you are," the deep voice of Dr. Benton boomed behind her.

Startled, she turned to see the older man standing next to another taller and much younger one wearing a hospital-issue white jacket.

"Sarah, I'd like you to meet Dr. David Wright. He's starting his fellowship here with our cardiothoracic surgery group this week."

Standing, Sarah held out her hand. As the new MD shook it she looked up into a striking pair of eyes that were an unusual blend of light green and gray, and an attack of déjà vu hit her as she took in the dark brown hair and the square chin that accompanied them. She was certain that she'd seen the face before, but where?

"Are you okay?" a warm, concerned voice asked. A voice she could swear she had heard before. Was it her imagination or had she met or seen this man before?

Sarah shook off the trace of an old memory that seemed just out of reach. Realizing she still held the new doctor's hand, she loosened her grip and withdrew her hand, then looked back into questioning eyes. Could she have made any more of a bad impression? The man had to think she was crazy. And maybe she was.

"I'm sorry," she said, as she tried to get her mind back on track, "I'm at least one cup of coffee behind my usual schedule this morning. It's nice to meet you Dr. Wright."

"Sarah's one of our nurse practitioners. I swear we wouldn't get anything done if we didn't have her. If you have any questions or needs, she'll be able to help you," said Dr. Benton. The gray-haired man looked down to his watch. "I hate to leave you, David, but I've got a budget meeting to get to."

With a heart that was beating way too fast, Sarah started for the door, anxious to excuse herself as well. Why was this man affecting her this way? Yes, he was a nice-looking man, but she met nice-looking men all the time and none of them had ever made her feel as if her heart was going to come out of her chest. No, it wasn't his good looks that were upsetting her, but there was something about the man that was ringing all her warning bells.

"I've got a great idea," Dr. Benton said,

"how about you show Dr. Wright around for the rest of the morning, Sarah?"

Sarah stopped. She should have seen this coming as soon as Dr. Benton had begun giving his excuses. The chief of the department was good at volunteering her time and there was no way she could get out of this without appearing rude. Besides, if Dr. Benton followed his normal course when he had an intern or new fellowship participant, she would be helping with a lot of Dr. Wright's day-to-day orientation. She pivoted and turned back toward the two men and forced a friendly smile on her face. Her working relationship with all the staff was important and if she was going to be spending a lot of time with the new doctor she didn't want to mess this one up, no matter how he made her feel.

"Of course," Sarah said. "I'm rounding right now, but I'd be glad to take you along with me."

"That would be great," the younger doctor said as his face lit up with a smile that was too bright for Sarah to comprehend at this time of the morning.

Sarah waited for him to catch up with her, and then started down the hallway toward the PCIC unit.

"Are you from Houston, Dr. Wright?" she asked as she gave him a sideways glance, looking for anything that would help her remember where she might have seen him before. Maybe she was wrong. But still, there was something inside her that recognized this man.

"Please, call me David," he said. "No, I'm from Alabama, though I did my residency just east of here, in Beaumont."

"What was your residency in?" she asked. Maybe she'd seen him at one of the many state conferences she had attended.

"It was in pediatric cardiothoracic surgery, but they didn't have a transplant program there so—" he held his arms up in the air, then shrugged "—here I am."

"Our pediatric transplant center is one

of the best in the country as I'm sure you know. It's always nice to see new doctors interested in the specialty," she said.

"Believe me, I'm very well aware of what a wonderful program you have here. I feel very lucky to have been given this opportunity with Dr. Benton. The residency in pediatric cardiac was great, but my main interest now is in transplantation. It's where I think I can make a real difference," he said. A shadow passed over his face, reminding her of a man from the past that she had never been able to forget. But then he blinked and the pain she had seen was gone.

She was being ridiculous continuing on this path. He couldn't be the man from the waiting room that day so long ago. David was much younger than the man she remembered.

But still…for just a second those haunted eyes—the color of fresh green pastures shrouded in the thick gray mist of early morning—had reminded her of a time she didn't want to remember. Not here. Not now.

"Well, we're glad to have you," Sarah said politely. She couldn't keep playing this game of detective. If she had met David somewhere she would eventually remember where. Till then she needed to concentrate on her job of helping him get acquainted with everything.

She stopped at the closed doors to the unit and swiped her badge, then waited for the doors to open.

They entered the unit and she headed straight to the nurses' station where only the unit coordinator was in attendance.

"Betsy, this is Dr. Wright. He's starting a fellowship with Dr. Benton and I'm going to be showing him around the unit today."

"Hello, Dr. Wright," Betsy greeted David, quickly taking the time to explain to him where the charts and miscellaneous equipment was kept in the unit.

Sarah picked up the chart with the records that had come along with a baby girl that had been transferred there during the night, turning to David once Betsy had finished.

"I want to start with a new patient we had flown in during the night. She was diagnosed at three days old with hypoplastic left heart syndrome after she became cyanotic. We have the results of the echocardiogram that was performed. It looks like the IV medications are working for now, but I want to see her first and have a talk with her parents," Sarah said as David joined her on her rounds through the unit.

"I'm glad they caught it this early. I've seen cases where it's only been diagnosed after the infant is critical and unstable," David said as they stopped at the door of a room where a young mother stood over a sleeping infant.

As they entered the room she saw a young man asleep on a cot that had been brought into the room as well, leaving her in no doubt that it had been a long night for this young family.

"Ms. Lawrence?" she asked as she held out her hand to the young woman. Her eyes were red and damp and Sarah's heart broke for the woman. She would never be able to forget the helplessness you felt as a mother unable to make your child whole again.

"My name is Sarah and I'm a nurse practitioner with the thoracic-cardio group, and this is Dr. Wright."

She watched as David shook the woman's hand and then led her to a group of chairs in the room.

"Shall we sit down?" he asked the young woman who looked close to collapsing.

"Let me wake my husband," the young mother said. "And please call me Maggie."

The young mother bent over and whispered into her husband's ear. When the couple joined them, Sarah began going over the tests that had been done on their daughter so far. Though she was sure the doctors had reviewed everything with them before their daughter had been transferred, Sarah knew that it was easy in these situations for parents to be overwhelmed with too much information. It was better to repeat the information they needed than to assume they had been informed.

"So, the IV medications that they've started Breanna on are working?" John, the young father, asked, looking hopefully across the room where his newborn daughter lay.

"For now, but it's only a temporary fix. Breanna still needs surgery and there will be more surgeries necessary later," David said.

As David went on to explain the procedures that were needed and the many surgeries that would be necessary, Sarah found herself impressed with how understanding and patient he seemed to be with the parents' questions and concerns.

Before they left the room, Sarah listened to the baby's heart and lungs, noting that even with the medications that were keeping the ductus open, the infant's color was still a sickly gray. She pulled out her phone and texted the cardiologist on call with her concerns, then used the computer at the bedside to order the tests that would be needed before they took the infant to surgery.

"I'm sorry. I haven't been officially assigned to the case, I shouldn't have taken over like that. I get a little carried away sometimes. It's just..." said David. "It's better that they know what they're up against from the beginning so that they can prepare themselves."

"We have a great team here and we stress the importance of making sure all our parents understand what is going on with their child, but sometimes they're in such denial that it just takes time for them to come to terms with their child's condition," she said. Sarah understood his frustration only too well. She remembered being on the other side of those conversations when her mind had been unable to wrap itself around what she was being told by the medical staff.

She forced the thoughts of those days away, and mentally shut the door to where she kept the memories of a life she'd had before locked away. There was only one place where she felt safe to take those memories out and it certainly wasn't here at the hospital. She'd always been very careful to keep her work life separate from the personal memories she had of this place.

"There's nothing that can prepare them for how their life is going to change. Right now it looks like they have a strong marriage. We can only hope that it will be up to the test that having a critically ill child brings," David said as they headed toward the next room.

Was that a hint of bitterness that Sarah heard? There was a story there, she was sure. Glancing over at David, she tried to catch a glimpse of the man she had seen earlier, the man with the haunted eyes. It seemed she wasn't the only one who had something she kept hidden away.

They made their way through the critical care unit and then continued down the acute pediatric cardiac floor, looking in on patients recovering from surgery and those who had been brought in for assessments for surgery or for placement on the transplant waiting list. They stopped at the room of a teenage boy, Jason, who had been brought in after collapsing on the baseball field at his high school a couple of days ago.

Sarah had tried to get the boy to talk to her on her last two visits, but he'd answered her with only one word responses then focused on his phone when she had tried to start a conversation with him.

"Jason's scheduled tomorrow to have a defibrillator implanted, but he's refused to agree to the procedure," she told David as they stopped outside the room.

"I know it would be best to have his

agreement, but the fact is that he's a minor so we only need his parents' consent," David said.

"Well, yes, but that's not the point. He's the one who's going to be living with this for the rest of his life." A point she had made to Dr. Benton the day before.

"Do you mind if I see him alone?" David asked as he moved toward the room. "I'll leave the door open so that you can hear."

"Give it your best shot," she said. "He's certainly not responding to me or Dr. Benton."

David rapped his knuckles on the door and entered leaving the door partially open as he had promised.

"Hey, Jason, my name is Dr. Wright."

Sarah wasn't surprised when she heard the boy answer with a grunt and the sound of the boy's computer keys continuing to click. So far it was teenager one. Dr. Wright zero.

"Today's my first day here on the unit

and I wanted to introduce myself," said David.

Another grunt came from the room now making it teenager two, Dr. Wright still zero, but she had to give it to David, he wasn't giving up.

"I'm a thoracic surgeon here to study transplantation," David said.

"I don't need a transplant," Jason said with an exaggerated sigh.

Sarah couldn't help but be impressed. That was more than she had been able to get out of the kid in the last two days. Still, from Jason's uninterested tone, she'd have to consider the point a tie.

"No, you don't," David said, his voice still patient. "Nice computer. The graphics are amazing."

"Yeah, they are. It's the best one I've ever had," Jason said. "You play any games?"

Sarah listened as David and Jason discussed computers and various aspects of computer gaming versus something called console games. After a couple minutes of computer terminology that she didn't understand, she heard David ask to see the teenager's computer.

"There are a couple videos I want to show you. It will explain a lot of what the doctors have been talking about as far as how they're going to fix your heart," David said.

As David explained the procedures alongside what they seemed to be reviewing on the computer, Sarah was amazed at the way the teenager was opening up with him. She would have to look into the videos available on the internet that could be used to educate their older patients.

"Is there anything on there that will tell me if I will be able to play baseball again?" Jason asked, and Sarah's heart sank. That was the real issue. His parents had explained to her that he had been playing baseball since he was able to hold a bat and it wasn't something that the boy would be able to give up on easily.

"There are actually some studies they've

done in relation to athletes and defibrillators, but as of now they are recommending that anyone with a defibrillator doesn't play most competitive sports," David said. She could hear the regret in his voice and hoped that Jason could hear it too. David understood the loss the boy was feeling at knowing that he was going to have to give up his favorite sport. "There are other sports that you can participate in though."

"But not baseball," Jason said, his voice so low now that Sarah could barely hear him.

A few minutes later David walked out of the room. Sarah had heard him promise Jason that he would be around early the next morning to see him before he was taken to surgery and it seemed that the boy was finally going to accept that the surgery was necessary.

"That was hard," David said as he joined Sarah in the hall.

"I know, but you did get him to agree to the surgery and you were honest with him," Sarah said as they headed to see the last patient of the morning. "What did you play?"

"Basketball," he said. "I had great dreams of making it big in the NBA."

"What happened?" she asked as she knocked on the door of the next patient.

"I reached five-eleven and stopped growing," he said, smiling as he turned his full attention to the little girl they found lying in the bed surrounded by stuffed animals.

Sarah looked down at the little blond girl whose breathing seemed even more labored today than it had the day before. As with a lot of pediatric heart patients, Lindsey was small for her ten years. The little girl looked up at her and smiled, those baby blue eyes hitting Sarah right in the heart. The two of them had been on such a long journey together over the past two and a half years as they had waited for a heart to become available. Lindsey been moved up recently on the waiting list so it was just a matter of waiting for a match with a donor heart. Only now Lindsey had been exposed to a respiratory virus that was making her heart work even harder.

She looked around the room and found the child alone as was often the case. Lindsey's mother, Hannah, was very young, and a single mom without any support, and had to work long hours to provide for her and Lindsey. But Lindsey was very sick right now and her mother needed to be there. Sarah would touch base with Hannah and give her an update so that she understood exactly how critical Lindsey's condition could become. Hannah had fought beside her daughter for so long, Sarah knew the young mother wouldn't give up now.

As David walked over to the bed to introduce himself to the little girl, Sarah joined the nurse who was charting on the computer at Lindsey's bedside.

"Has Pulmonary been in today?" Sarah asked.

"Yes, Dr. Lorten wants to do a bronchoscopy, but I haven't been able to get Hannah to give us consent," the nurse said.

"I'll call her," Sarah said. Then crouching down on the floor next to Lindsey's bed, she asked, "How are you feeling, kiddo?" She pushed the child's blond curls off her forehead and was relieved to feel it cool. No fever. At least that was a good sign.

"I'm not going to make it to see the horses this week, am I?" Lindsey asked.

"Horses?" asked David. He'd pulled a chair up beside Lindsey's bed while Sarah had been talking with Kim.

Lindsey turned her blue eyes toward him and for the first time in the last week she saw the little girl's eyes come alive.

"Oh, yes," Lindsey said. "Sarah has lots of pretty horses. I've seen pictures of them all. Maple is my favorite. Sarah let me name her myself when she first got her."

"And Maple will be waiting to see you as soon as you get better," Sarah said as she squeezed the little girl's hand in hers. "I'll tell you what—when I get home I'll take a picture of Maple for you and I'll bring it in tomorrow."

"I have to see this horse with a name like Maple," David said as he gave Lindsey a smile. The little girl's face turned pink and Sarah knew it wasn't from a fever. It looked like Lindsey might have her first crush, which was so sweet to see that Sarah couldn't help but smile up at the man who had made her special little girl happy when she was so sick.

She listened as Lindsey explained the therapy program Sarah ran at her father-in-law's ranch teaching young cardiac patients from the community how to ride. Or if their medical condition wouldn't allow them to participate in the riding lessons they could interact with the special therapy horses kept on the ranch. Sarah was proud of The Henderson Memorial horse therapy program that she had founded. Working with the children at the ranch wasn't only good for them, it had also been good for her.

"That sounds like a lot of fun," David said to the little girl.

"You can go too. Lots of times the doctors volunteer to help. Can he go, Sarah?" asked Lindsey.

"Of course he can come," Sarah answered. "And as soon as you get better, I'll take you out there to see Maple."

"I don't have any experience with horses, but I definitely know someone who would be interested in seeing them," David said as he gave Sarah a questioning look.

"We'd be happy to have them. We run the program on the second Saturday of the month and all the staff is welcome," Sarah said. A smile lit David's face and she couldn't help wondering who this someone was. A wife? She looked down at his left hand and saw that he wasn't wearing a ring. Maybe a girlfriend? It wouldn't be surprising that a man like David had someone special in his life.

As they left the room Sarah texted Hannah and asked her to call as soon as she had a minute. She didn't want to scare the girl's mother but she did need to get consent from Hannah and tell her that Lindsey's condition was getting worse. Hannah needed to know.

"How long has she been waiting?" David asked as they headed back to the doctor's workroom.

"Five years. She's been in and out, though mostly in, of here for the last two and a half years," Sarah said.

"Family issues?" David asked.

"Hannah's young and a single parent. I know this had been hard on her and I worry about her. She's been through a lot with Lindsey. She couldn't have been more than nineteen or twenty when Lindsey was born. When Lindsey gets a heart transplant—" she refused to consider that there was the possibility that the little girl wouldn't get a donor heart "—it's going to be a lot more responsibility."

"I hope for that child's sake that her mother is up for the job, but an overabundance of toys and the lack of a parent present is a sign... Let's just say I've had some experience as far as missing-in-action parents. It's a lot harder to be the parent at the bedside than the one that sends the prettiest packages." Again the hint of bitterness she heard in David's voice surprised her.

"Hannah's not like that. It will be a lot for her to handle, but she'll do it," Sarah asserted.

"About your ranch," David started as they turned back toward the nursing station.

"David? David Wright? Is that you?" Melody, one of the older staff nurses said as she jumped up from her seat and came around the desk to the two of them. "It is you. How's Davey doing? I've thought about him so much over the last few years."

"Mel! I didn't know if you still worked here or not. I meant to ask Dr. Benton, but

I haven't had a chance," David said as he beamed down at the gray-haired nurse. "Davey's great. I'll have to bring him up to see you one day when I'm off."

Sarah watched as the nurse turned around and announced to the other staff members that were looking curiously at the three of them, "David was here with his son, was it three years ago now?"

Sarah's heart stuttered then sped up to a dangerous rate as she waited for David's answer. Had she been wrong to dismiss that feeling of familiarity? Was this truly the man she'd seen over three years ago in the waiting room?

"Davey's 'new heart birthday' was three years in January," she heard David say.

That was all the confirmation she needed. It was him she remembered seeing.

The shock sent her spinning backward toward another time. A time when her perfect life had ended, only it hadn't. Life hadn't been that kind. Instead it had been heartbreaking and life shattering, made only bearable because of the man standing in front of her now.

Suddenly she was back in that waiting room, running from the terrible news the doctors had just given her and hiding from a family that would be as devastated as she was at the news that her little boy's brain had lost the ability to function. How could she face them with this news? Then she had seen the dark-haired man hunched over in his seat appearing to bear a burden just as heavy as her own. Immediately she had felt a connection to him, a compassion that only someone who was traveling the same path as she could feel.

But was David really that man? The man she had seen that night in the waiting room, the one who had broken down when the organ transplant case manager had told him that they might have a heart for his son, the one that she had wondered about for the last three years, the one who may have been given back his son because of the gift of her own son's heart?

It had to be more than just a coincidence that this man's son had been given a heart in this hospital around the same time of her son's accident. Around the same time that she had chosen to donate her own son's organs. A decision she'd made because of that man in the waiting room.

It had been David's eyes that had first sparked her memories of him, but now she could see that there was more. While he certainly looked much younger than the defeated man she had seen back then, the build and dark hair matched what she remembered of that night.

Sarah forced herself to stand there while the rest of the staff excitedly asked him questions concerning his son and his recovery. While the staff knew that she had lost her husband and son due to a car accident, Houston General was a big facility. She had been working on the adult surgical floor at the time of the accident and since her transfer to the pediatric cardiology service she had never discussed the donation of her own little boy's organs with the staff here. It was too personal and still too painful.

And what did she do now? What was she supposed to say to a man who had helped make the hardest decision in her life? How was she supposed to work next to David and never mention that time in her life when just looking at him brought back such difficult memories for her?

There had been days she had wished she had died in the car crash along with Kolton and Cody, but then she would think of that young father who'd been so desperate for a heart for his son.

Later, when she realized she wanted to do more to help families like that young man's, it had taken only one trip through the pediatric cardiac unit for her to know this was where she was needed, where she could help the critical children that waited for a new life with their families. She'd finished her nurse practitioner program and found a place in Dr. Benton's practice. And now the man who had influenced her life so much was here on her unit.

And what about his son, Davey? She'd always imagined that it had been her son who had saved the son of the man in the waiting room. Knowing that David's son had received a heart transplant back then made the possibility feel only more real. Now she had been given an opportunity to find out if she had been right all along.

As the rest of the staff started to disburse back to their patients, she pulled herself into the present only to find that some of the younger nurses were giving the new doctor more than just a friendly smile. Not that she could blame them for their interest. Dr. David Wright was a very good-looking man with his dark brown hair curling around his face, those striking eyes, and a smile full of laughter as he talked to Mel.

But there was more to the man than his

looks. She had immediately recognized that when she had first seen him. He had a strong, competent look to him that had quickly put the patients and their families at ease. And she remembered the way he had dealt with the news that there might be a last hope for his son. The anguish in his face had matched hers as she'd mourned the loss of hope for her own. He'd openly shed tears at the news that his son might be getting a new heart and still the man hadn't appeared weak.

Mentally shaking herself, she forced herself to put the old memories behind her again. It was not going to be easy to keep those memories away with David here, but she had to remember that it was the here and now that was important. Her past life was over, and she had patients that relied on her now. These were the children she was responsible for now. Later, when she could be alone, she'd take the time to deal with all of this and what it could mean for her.

She watched as Dr. Benton walked down the hall toward them and then as he and David walked away together. She had so many questions that she was desperate to find a way to ask, to tell him to wait so that she could ask the one question that was circling around and around in her head. It was a question that at some point she would have to ask, but it would have to wait.

Is the heart of my little boy, my Cody, beating in your son's chest?

CHAPTER TWO

DAVID PUT ONE of the cups of coffee he'd purchased at the trendy café across from the hospital on the desk in front of Sarah.

"What's this for?" Sarah asked as she looked up at him, those deep brown eyes questioning. It was a look he'd seen a lot lately when she looked at him. It was as if that intelligent mind of hers was trying to solve a complex puzzle, and for some reason he had a feeling that he was that puzzle.

"It's to say thank you. If it wasn't for you I'd have been buried in all this paperwork. I knew there was a lot of paperwork involved with the assessments for the transplant patients, but I never imagined that there would be this much," he said.

"Really? I guess I assumed that because

you had been through this firsthand that you'd know all about the mountains of paperwork," Sarah said. And there was that look again.

Was that what she was curious about? It wasn't that he didn't understand why she would be curious about what he had gone through. After working with her for the last week, he had quickly discovered that she had a very inquiring mind, and with working on one side of the transplant process it was only normal for her to want to know what it was like on the other side.

"I'm sorry, I didn't mean to pry," Sarah said, then looked back to the computer screen in front of her, her golden-tan cheeks turning a pretty pink with a blush that he found surprisingly charming. The Sarah that he had been working with didn't seem like the type of woman that would be so easily embarrassed, but there was always more to a person that what you first saw. If anyone should know that, he should. He'd thought he had known his ex-wife until their son had been born and everything in their life had changed.

"It's okay, Sarah. I don't mind talking about it, most parts at least," he said, then regretted that he had added the afterthought. He had no reason to think that any of her questions would deal with the breakup of his marriage.

"Are you sure?" she asked.

"I'm sure," David said.

He took his chair next to her and waited. It was almost as if he could see the gears in her mind turning as she seemed to struggle with her question.

"What was wrong with Davey? Why did he need the transplant?" Sarah asked.

"Davey was diagnosed with hypoplastic left heart syndrome not long after he was born. It hadn't been caught on ultrasound so it was a shock. There were a lot of surgeries before it was decided that a transplant would be necessary. There wasn't anything else they could do for him."

"I'm sorry. That had to be hard for you and your wife."

Deep brown eyes seemed to bore into his, or was it just that he felt uncomfortable discussing the situation with his ex-wife with Sarah?

"And he's okay now?" Sarah asked.

"He's great. He's done a lot of growing in the last three years. I keep a close watch on him and he still has a lot of follow-up testing that's necessary, but so far he's not shown any signs of rejection over the past three years."

David watched her as Sarah bit down on her lip, an act that caught way too much of his attention.

"Can I ask you one more question?" she asked.

"Sure," David said as he forced his eyes away from lips that looked way too dangerous right then.

"What did it feel like when you learned that there was a heart available for your son?" she asked, her eyes never wavering from his.

This was not the question he had expected. He had thought maybe she would want to know about the impact that a sick child had on someone's life or how he had gotten through the awful waiting period. But this? That moment had to have been the most emotional moment of his life. How did you explain the feeling of being lifted from a pit of despair and given the chance of a new life?

"It's hard to explain," he said, not knowing where to start. Though it might seem like an easy question to answer to Sarah, it was far from it. Someone would have to understand where Davey was in his life at that time. "Davey had so many surgeries before he was finally put on the transplant list. With each surgery, I kept thinking this will be the last one. But it never was, and when he was almost two it was determined that the only thing that would save him would be a transplant. I knew the odds that he would receive one in time were against us. By the time I brought Davey here, his heart was failing and we were getting to the point where I was going to have to make some hard decisions on his care. I'd almost given up. I had walked out into the waiting room knowing that if there wasn't a miracle I would lose my little boy within the next few days. Then one of the organ procurement staff found me and told me that there was a good chance that Davey would be getting a heart very soon. Learning that there was a heart available for my son was the happiest moment of my life. I don't have another experience to compare it to. To have that hope of a future for your child when you are at the point of giving up is unimaginable. It was like going from the lowest point in your life to the happiest in two point five seconds and not knowing if you should laugh or cry."

"I'm glad that it worked out that way, that you were given that chance."

* * *

This was it. This was the moment she had been obsessed with over the last week. All she had to do was explain that she had been there that night and that she had suspicions that the case manager that night had been talking about her son when she had told David that there could be a heart available. All she had to do was open her mouth and the words would come, she knew they would.

"Hey, Sarah, Hannah's here and wanted to know if you had a second to talk to her," Melody said from the doorway.

She'd missed her chance.

Turning away from David she stood and headed toward the door before turning back. "Didn't you say you'd like to meet Lindsey's mother?" she asked.

"That's okay," David said, "I'm scheduled in surgery with Dr. Benton this afternoon."

"Okay," she said, then turned again toward the door before stopping a second time. "Did you say you wanted to come out to the ranch? This Saturday is therapy day for the kids enrolled in the program if you want to come and bring your son."

"Yeah, Davey would love that."

She could feel his searching eyes on her as she left the room. Instead of coming clean with David, she had just managed to make him think she was nosy. There had to be a better way to go about this. If only she didn't feel that gut-wrenching pain when she thought of that night maybe she could. She'd asked David to share his personal experiences with her, but she'd been unable to share with him her own experiences that day.

She'd been working one on one with David for a week now helping him to understand her side of the cardiac practice and she'd been impressed with how well he interacted with both the young patients and their parents. He'd been up-front with the parents when they'd had concerns about their children's diagnosis and risks of the many procedures that were necessary. She had no doubt that if it was David in her position that he would have come right out and told her.

But he hadn't been through what she had been through that night, she reminded herself. His child had survived that night, hers hadn't. Either way, she had to tell him. The next time she had an opportunity to tell David she'd do it, no matter how much it hurt.

David pulled his car off the highway and stared down the long dirt road. He'd been driving for almost an hour and had started to think he was lost.

"Are we there?" his son asked, trying to strain his neck to look over from his booster seat in the back of the car.

David looked at the metal sign hanging over the road that swung back and forth with the wind. He hadn't expected anything this big when Lindsey had been telling him about the horses Sarah had at her house, but from the size of the pastures that ran on both sides of the road he could see he had been mistaken. He looked back up at the sign that read "Henderson's Horse Farm."

"I think we are," he answered his son.

He eased his car down the clay dirt road until he saw the large stables surrounded by a high white livestock fence. He parked the car beside an old gray pickup truck covered in red dust and a new SUV that along with his car looked totally out of place.

After opening the back door to get his son out, he fought with the seat buckle as his son tried to help.

"Hurry, Daddy, I want to see the horses," Davey said as he pulled against the buckled strap.

"I know, son, but we're not going to get there any sooner if you don't let me get this buckle undone," David said. Somehow he could perform surgery on the smallest of hearts, but the talent for unbuckling the car seat was something he had never been able to achieve. Finally, he freed his son and he watched as Davey ran toward the open door of the stable.

"Woe, slow down partner," David said as he grabbed his son's hand, "we talked about this. We don't run where there are big horses around, do we?"

By the time they had entered the door, Davey had stopped trying to pull against his dad and slowed to a stop as soon as he saw the other children and adults in the building. As Sarah made her way over to them, his son had grabbed him behind his leg and was trying to hide behind him. Davey had a tendency to be shy when he first met new people, but he was too inquisitive for it to last very long.

"Davey, this is Mrs. Henderson. She's the one who invited us to come see the horses," David said as he tried to pry his son from behind him. "Remember, I told you she had a horse named Maple."

"That's a funny name for a horse,"

Davey said, peaking around his father's leg at Sarah.

Unlike the always neatly dressed Sarah he was used to seeing, this Sarah wore a long-tailed chambray shirt that looked two sizes too big over jeans that had almost faded to white. Jeans that were tucked into a pair of scarred brown cowboy boots. Her hair, usually piled atop her head, was hanging down past her shoulders in thick brown waves and her warm brown eyes seemed to be captivated by his son who had finally come out from behind him, though he still hung onto David's legs.

"Maybe she's a funny horse. Do you want to go see her?" she asked as she bent down and held out her hand to his five-year-old son.

David followed the two of them over to where four other children and a short weathered man seemed to be studying a dark brown horse that stood in a rectangular stall.

"This is Davey," Sarah said as she started to introduce his son to all the other children.

"Hi, I'm Jack Henderson," the man said as he held out his hand. David put his age around sixty and figured this couldn't be Sarah's husband. He shook Jack's hand and then the man turned toward Davey.

"Hi, Davey. I'm Miss Sarah's father-in-law, Mr. Jack. Did I hear you say that our Maple is a funny horse?" the man asked as he bent down so that he could talk to Davey.

"I said it was a funny name. I didn't know horses could be funny," Davey said.

"Well, horses have all kinds of personalities, just like people. How about I introduce you to some of them?" Jack said as he held his hand to Davey. Davey stared up at him with eyes that pleaded for his dad to let him go explore the other stalls.

"You can go, but remember what I said about running and no leaving the stable without me," David said, then watched as his son headed off with the older man toward the end of the stalls. He could tell by how the man had interacted with Davey that he had spent some time around children, but Davey could be a handful at times and he really didn't like letting him go off with strangers. Hearing a loud snort, he turned to see Sarah opening a stall and leading out the large brown horse.

"Josh, you can take Maddie but stay in the north paddock where I can see you," she said while handing the reins over to an older teenage boy, who took the horse and led him out of the stable.

He watched as she handed the reins of a smaller horse to a young nurse he had seen at the hospital, who took the horse and the other three children out another side door. As Sarah walked toward him, he was aware of how much she looked like she belonged here, while he felt totally out of his element. He forced his eyes away from Sarah and back to Davey.

"He'll be fine," Sarah said as she appeared at his side, "Jack will watch him."

"I know," he said, though he couldn't help but check on the progress his son and the older man were making as they seemed to be stopping at each stall.

"I'm so glad you made it," Sarah said as she looked around the stable. "What do you think?"

"It's definitely not what I was expecting," he said, "I was thinking you had a couple of horses in your backyard. This is amazing."

"It is, isn't it," she said. Her eyes lit up with her smile and it was easy to see how much she loved the ranch. "It's a lot of work, but Jack has a small staff that helps with the horses and keeps up the grounds."

"Are all the horses yours?" David asked as he looked at the horses still in their stalls as they walked toward the door where the group of children had gone. He took a look back behind him and saw that

Davey was still occupied with Jack as they continued going from horse to horse.

"Only three of them are mine, but we board a few for friends, or Jack does, but most of them are for breeding. This is all Jack's. I just help when I can. He's been great about letting me base a therapy program here. The kids love it out here and after spending as much time as they do inside hospital walls, it's good for them to spend time outside. I give some private lessons to the kids from the hospital that are interested and cleared medically by their doctors," she said.

"I'm impressed," he said. "And your husband? I thought I might meet him today. Is he not a horse person?" Though how he couldn't be if he was raised among all these beautiful animals he couldn't imagine.

"My husband, Kolton, passed away. We started the therapy program in memory of him," Sarah said, turning away from him and stopping to rub the neck of a beautiful white horse that was nudging her with his head. David stood and watched the two of them as he tried to think of something to say. But what was there to say? She was so young to have lost her husband. He had noticed that she didn't mention anything about her family, but he had assumed that she was just a private person when it came to her home life.

"I'm so sorry, Sarah. I didn't know," he said. It sounded so inadequate.

"It's okay. It's not something I talk about. It's in the past," Sarah said as she continued to talk quietly to the horse in front of her, which seemed to comfort both of them.

"And this, Davey, is Sugar," Jack said as he and David's son walked up behind them making it easy to change the subject from one that he could see made Sarah uncomfortable.

"So she's named Sugar because she's sweet?" Davey asked the older man. David could see the wonder in his son's eyes as he stared up at the large white horse. He'd heard of people getting horse fever and he could understand them now. He was sure it would be easy to fall in love with any one of the animals.

"She's named Sugar because she was the sweetest gift I was ever given," said Sarah. "Do you want to pet her?"

David tensed as Sarah lifted his son up on her hips and showed him the proper way to touch a horse and explained to him how Sugar liked her neck rubbed in long strokes. He'd been a little apprehensive about bringing Davey around the big horses, but after talking with some of the nurses at work, he'd learned that Sarah had a good reputation for working safely with the patients from the hospital. Still, he'd have to buy Davey a safety helmet if he was going to spend more time here. And from the look on Davey's face, they would be back.

Looking over at the majestic animal, he had to admit he would like to learn more about the horses himself. Maybe this was something the two of them could do together; and Sarah was right, the fresh air was good for children.

"Can I touch her?" he asked Sarah.

She gave him a smile and a nod and he reached out to the horse and rubbed its neck. It was easy to see why his son enjoyed this as the horse leaned her head against him.

"I'm thinking this horse definitely deserves its name. What do you think, Davey?" he asked his son.

"You should see the big black one down there," his son said as he pointed to the other end of the building. "His name is Thunder. Mr. Jack says it's because he makes a really loud noise when he runs. Mr. Jack said I might get to ride him some day when I'm bigger. You want to see him?"

Letting Davey down onto the floor, Sarah explained where they would be and David let his son pull him down to where the large black horse whose temperament seemed to match its name stood with a look that seemed to dare the two of them to come any closer. He knew immediately that he would never be comfortable with his son riding such a big horse. As his son rattled off the names of other horses, they headed out to where Sarah was working with the other children.

"That was great, Ryan. Take him around one more time. Loosen up on the reins a bit," Sarah said as she directed a boy that couldn't have been over ten. "There, you see. She's not fighting against you when the bit's looser."

David leant against a fence and watched her as she took time with each child, making sure they felt comfortable with the horse as well as that the horse felt comfortable with them. He'd learned so much about Sarah today. He had assumed that Sarah was married after she had mentioned that she ran the therapy program with her father-in-law. He'd never imagined that she had lost a husband. Sometimes he forgot that he wasn't the only one who had things in their past that they didn't want to discuss with others.

When Jack returned with a small brown pony, he watched Davey's eyes light up and there was no telling him that he couldn't take a ride around the paddock on him. He pulled out his phone and started a search for a helmet with a good safety rating.

Sarah watched as Jack worked with Davey on the pony he had brought up from the small paddock they had behind the house. She could barely pull her eyes away from the child that looked so much like his father with his dark hair and those beautiful eyes. He had been shy at first, hiding behind his father. Cody had been the same way when he had first met strangers, though like Davey the shyness was short-lived. She couldn't help but smile when the little boy started giggling over something that Jack had said to him, though inside she felt a sting of pain with the memory of her own son who had loved spending time with his grandfather.

She hadn't been surprised when her father-in-law had been drawn to the small boy. Though Jack rarely showed his grief of losing his only son and the only grand-child he would ever have, she knew that working with the kids from the hospital helped him as much as it did her and the kids. And though smaller than Cody would have been at Davey's age, the boy's excited nature around the horses couldn't help but remind them both of how excited three-year-old Cody had always been when his grandfather had walked him around the stable telling him about all of the horses he would be able to ride once he got big-ger. Only Cody had never had the chance to get big enough to ride one of the horses.

"Thanks again, for letting us come," David said. "Davey will be talking about this for a long time."

"I'm glad he's enjoying it. He and Jack seem to be having fun. Let's give them a little more time," she said as she climbed the wood fence that circled the paddock so that she could see the little boy better.

As she had worked with the rest of the kids, she'd given a lot of thought about what she was going to say to David. A part of her desperately wanted to know if there was a possibility that her son's donated heart had been given to his son while another part just wanted to enjoy the day sitting beside David as they watched his son taking his ride. Once the rest of the children had left, she'd decided that taking small steps to see what she could learn would be the best course for now. She knew she was being a coward in not telling David just yet about the chance that Davey had received her son's heart, but she also knew that David was a private man and she couldn't just hit him with that information until she had an idea about how he would take it. She didn't want things to become strange between the two of them. They would still have to work together no matter what she learned about Davey's heart.

And she'd have to tell him about losing Cody and right now watching the healthy little boy that Davey had grown up to be, she didn't want to face the pain of the past. But she could use this opportunity to learn more about Davey.

"I saw Massey in the office with Dr. Benton for her checkup last week. She told me that you were giving her private lessons here?" he asked. She watched as he climbed the fence then slung his own legs across the top board.

"I offer to give all our patients private lessons when they're well enough to take them. She was cleared to start lessons six months after her transplant last year. She's doing really well. Are you thinking about letting Davey take lessons?" she asked. She watched as Davey broke out in laughter again. It was amazing how after everything the little boy had been through, he was still such a happy child. From things David had said she knew that he had worked hard to let Davey live as much of a normal life as possible. She couldn't help but wonder where Davey's mother fit into their life.

"Maybe, someday, but I was thinking maybe it would be good for me to take them first. That way I would know the risks," he said as he joined her in watching his laughing son.

"That would probably be good for you. It might make you feel better to know how I teach, that is if you want me to teach him."

"It's not that I don't trust you, it's just…" David looked over at her as he rubbed the back of his neck with one hand as he held on to the fence with the other. "Okay, maybe I'm a little protective, but it's not personal. Besides, I can't have my son outdoing me."

"I understand, David," she said. She couldn't help but think of how Kolton had made fun of how protective she had been of Cody around the horses. "I'd be glad to give you some lessons, but I have to tell you that I'm used to teaching kids, not adults."

"The children you teach probably know a lot more than I do about horses. It would probably be good if we just start off with the basics like you would with them," David said.

The two of them sat and watched as Jack explained the parts of the saddle to Davey. He had always liked to start with the basics of horsemanship too.

"Can I ask you a question? You don't have to answer if you don't want to," Sarah said. Now that the two of them knew each other better she was hoping that she wouldn't offend him with one of the questions that had nagged at her from the time she'd learned that David was a single parent.

"Let me guess, you're wondering about Davey's mother." While he didn't seem upset by his comment, she could still tell that it wasn't something he liked to talk about.

"I'm sorry if..."

"It's okay. It's not the first time I've been asked about Lisa. There's not that many single dads raising a child who's had a heart transplant. Questions about my ex are kind of natural. Lisa... She didn't really understand what we were up against at first. I tried to explain it to her, but she...she seemed to think I was making too much of Davey's heart defect. She had this idea that there would be a surgery and then we'd get back to our lives," David said.

"A lot of times that's as far as a parent can think ahead. They're not really ready to deal with the future. They've made plans for their children's lives and then everything changes and their whole world falls apart. It's understandable that it might have taken some time for your wife to understand." Sarah knew only too well how it felt when suddenly your world was upended.

"Once Lisa realized what life with Davey was going to be like, she took off," David said. Anger dripped from every word, but if what he said was true, she couldn't blame him for being angry. How could any woman leave their child when they were the most vulnerable? She could understand why David didn't like to drag out memories of his wife. It had to be painful for him. And here she had been the one to cause him to relive those memories while she hadn't had the courage to share her own with him.

"I'm sorry, I know that couldn't have been easy for you. I know it might seem strange that I'm asking all these questions, it's just that I need to tell you…"

Suddenly Jack and Davey joined them at the fence, chattering animatedly. For a few minutes Sarah had forgotten that the two of them weren't alone. Now a bittersweet feeling filled her as she saw the light in her father-in-law's eyes. A light that had been missing for so long now. She looked down at the little boy at Jack's side. A miniature copy of David.

Jumping down from the fence she and David followed as Davey and Jack headed back to the stables, where Davey insisted on saying goodbye to all the horses individually.

And later as she watched David load a reluctant Davey into his car seat, she found herself pitying the little boy's mother who was missing so much by not being there with her son. She couldn't help but wonder about the woman who had walked away from a man like David. He had everything to offer a woman but somehow it seemed that hadn't been enough for his ex-wife.

And that was the problem when you became too involved in someone's life. Her obsession with knowing if Davey had her son's heart had her becoming more and more involved with David. She needed to mind her own business, but that was hard to do when she felt that her and David's lives had somehow been tied together that night three years ago. Still, she had no business being concerned about David's private life. It wasn't like she was interested in the man, at least not *that* way. She hadn't thought about another man since she lost her husband. She had accepted that that part of her life was over when she had buried her husband and son. There was no reason for her to waste her time thinking of the good-looking doctor. His being married or divorced wasn't important. The only thing she was interested in was learning more about Davey and finding out if he had been the recipient of her son's heart.

A tiny voice inside her head called her a liar, but she refused to listen. She and David had a good relationship as co-workers, and they were becoming friends and that was all the two of them could ever be. How that friendship would fare when he learned that she had been keeping her suspicions concerning his son's heart to herself she didn't know, but she would have to face it soon. She couldn't keep living this way, dodging every opportunity to come clean with David.

She made herself a promise that she would come clean with him the next time they were alone. She would open up to David about everything and somehow the two of them would work through this together.

Sarah walked into the unit early Monday morning to find the nurses rushing around the room of one of the toddlers that she had been involved with assessing for the transplant waiting list several weeks earlier. The eighteen-month-old had been diagnosed with cardiomyopathy are there had been little hope that there would be an available match in time to save him as he had been deteriorating at a faster pace than they had expected. And unfortunately, the little boy had antibodies that they knew would make it even harder to find a donor match. The call that there had been a match found had come unexpectedly and both the staff and the parents were thrilled.

Sarah took a minute to say hi to Tyler's parents then started her examination of the little boy.

"Hey," she heard from behind her. Turning she saw that David had arrived. Dressed in scrubs and with his hair bushed out wildly around his head, he looked as excited as a kid on Christmas morning.

"Hey," she said, relieved that David seemed to be as comfortable with her as he had been before she had started prying into his business.

She introduced David to Tyler's parents as they waited for the operating team to arrive to take the toddler to the operating room.

"How far out is the team?" she asked as she watched Tyler's parents say goodbye. Their fear for their son was almost palpable in the room and she and David stepped out of the room to give the family some privacy.

"They called a few minutes ago and they were loading the plane then. It's an hour flight. They're as surprised as the rest of us that they found a match for Tyler this soon," David said.

She saw David look back into the room. Was he remembering how he had felt the day he had turned his own son over to the operating team as she was remembering the day they had taken her son away to the operating room? She had learned to accept the loss of her son and over the years she had seen many young patients who had survived because of the gift of life another grieving mother and father had helped give, but there were times that the pain refused to stay buried. She would never regret that her son had been able to save other children, but it didn't ease the loss of her son.

They both turned and watched as the

OR team arrived and the little boy was taken off on the stretcher. As David left to follow Tyler into the operating room, she watched as the couple began to gather their belongings so they could join the rest of their family in the waiting room.

Sarah, like the rest of the staff on the unit watched the clock constantly for the next few hours. News that the heart had been delivered and the surgery was going well so far filtered down through unofficial channels. As the hours passed and they waited for news that Tyler was coming off the bypass machine, Sarah forced herself to make her rounds. She'd stopped by Jason's room to find the teenager preparing to be discharged home. Unlike the boy she had seen the week before, he now was willing to talk to her as she discussed his post-op care and his need to return for a follow-up appointment.

After checking the clock again when she left Jason's room she turned and headed down to Lindsey's room. She'd checked on the little girl on and off during the weekend and she'd been happy to learn that there had been some improvement in her condition. Opening the door to her room she was greeted with a smiling Lindsey who sat up on her bed playing with a pink unicorn with a long flowing tail.

"Now, that is a pretty horse," Sarah said as she moved some of the child's other toys off the bedside chair so that she could sit down.

"It's a unicorn. My momma brought it for me this weekend," Lindsey said. "Isn't she pretty?"

"She is," Sarah said as she reached over and stroked the long rainbow-colored main. "Maybe we could dye Maple's hair this color."

Lindsey laughed, and then covered her mouth as she coughed. Sarah bent over and listened to her lungs with her stethoscope, then moved back to her chair.

"I'm much better," she said to Sarah. "I

told my momma that I might get out of the hospital this week."

Sarah let her hands run through Lindsey's long curls. She hoped that Hannah had been able to see that the child was being overly optimistic. Even with the improvement from the antibiotics she was getting it would be several days before they would move her out of the critical care unit. Lindsey's condition was just too fragile to not take every precaution.

Her phone beeped and she looked down to find a message from Tyler's parents. After she gave Lindsey the promised picture of Maple, Sarah headed down a floor to where Tyler's parents waited in the surgical waiting room.

"Oh, Sarah," Tyler's mother said as she rounded the corner and found both the child's parents standing in the hallway. "They said they would give us an update in an hour but that was over an hour and a half ago and no one has been out. The last update they gave us they said they were almost ready to take Tyler off the bypass machine. Can you find out what's going on?"

"Let's go over here," Sarah said as she led the distraught mother back over to the area of the waiting room where she recognized some of Tyler's other family members.

"I tried to tell her that they were just running a little behind," Tyler's father said reassuringly, though Sarah saw the way the man's hands trembled as he gently rubbed his wife's back.

"Let me go see what I can find out," Sarah said, praying that nothing had gone wrong in the OR.

Before she could turn from the couple, though, she heard the voice of Dr. Benton as he entered the waiting room, David just behind him. The smile on both their faces told her all she needed to know.

As Dr. Benton discussed the surgery with Tyler's parents, Sarah walked over to where David stood.

"So how did it go?" Sarah asked, as the two of them moved away from the group that surrounded Dr. Benton.

"It was amazing," David said, "that moment when we removed the heart was one of the scariest moments of my surgical career so far, but after the new heart was attached and we waited for the new heart to start up…then that first beat and then another. It was like experiencing a miracle."

"Weren't you?" Sarah asked as she smiled up at him. They headed back to the doctors' workroom where they could start requesting all the lab work and other tests that would need to be done on their newest transplant recipient. Sarah was impressed with the questions David had concerning the care Tyler would receive over the next twenty four hours. She had met many doctors in her years working as a nurse and then as a nurse practitioner and she felt that she had enough experience with both really good doctors and some not-so-good doctors to be able to tell the difference.

She was already sure that David would be one of the best doctors due partly to his enthusiasm and partly to the empathy he showed for his patients.

While most of the doctors she had worked with showed their patients and their families' empathy, David had experienced exactly what these families were going through which made him able to help them in ways that other doctors wouldn't understand.

"By the way, I was thinking maybe I could start those riding lessons next week. That is if you have the time," David asked as he set a cup of coffee on the desk in front of her.

They had fallen into a pattern of working together where the two of them ended each day discussing their plans for the next day. She was going to miss this when David finished his time learning the part of the practice that she handled.

"Sure," Sarah said. "How about next Saturday? I'll check with Jack, but if he doesn't have anything scheduled I'm sure he'd be happy to watch Davey for you. That is if you are okay with that." Her father-in-law had mentioned the young boy several times in the last few days and she knew he had enjoyed the time he's spent with Davey.

"Jack seems like a nice guy," David said. "If you don't mind me asking, does he have any other children?"

Sarah knew that David was being only curious about a man that his son had enjoyed spending time with, but that didn't keep her from feeling the pain that was always present when she discussed her husband.

"Kolton, my husband, was an only child," she said.

"I'm sorry. It's easy to see how good Jack is with kids. He would have made a great grandfather," David said.

This was the opportunity for her to tell David about Cody. If she could get through this maybe she would be able to approach the subject of Davey's donated heart.

Little steps. Just take this little step and everything will be okay.

"He was a great grandfather to our son, Cody. When we lost Cody and Kolton, it was really hard on him," she said.

"Oh, Sarah, I'm so sorry. I didn't know," David said. He reached out and covered her hand with his. A small gesture but somehow it helped ease the pain that always came when she was forced to talk about the loss she had experienced.

"It's not something I talk about. It's hard, you know?" she said. She took a deep breath and forced the air out.

"I'm sorry. I can't imagine what you must have gone through," David said as his hand tightened on hers. "How long ago did this happen?"

"Sometimes it feels like it was a long time ago and others it feels like it was just yesterday, but it was actually just over three years ago January," she said. Would the time ring a bell with him? Was there a possibility that he would put things together without her having to tell him?

"There was an accident, a car accident," she continued. Just that one statement drained her. There was a reason she didn't discuss this with other people. It was still too raw. She wondered if she would ever be able to speak about her son and husband without feeling that way. Her mother had wanted her to go to a counselor, but she hadn't been able to make herself go even after her mother had made an appointment for her.

"I'm sorry, Sarah. And I've sat here telling you how hard it is to live with the emotional rollercoaster of waiting for a heart donor," David said before he withdrew his hand from hers.

She knew David was feeling uncomfortable now, which was another reason for not discussing the loss of her family with others. The conversation always became awkward later.

"If you ever need to talk, just let me know. I can be a good listener," he said, then gave her a small smile before he returned his attention to the computer screen and she knew her chance to tell him everything she needed to was gone.

CHAPTER THREE

DAVID WAS UP early Saturday morning at his son's demand. Davey had been so excited the night before when he learned that they would be going back to see his friend, Jack, that he hadn't been able to sleep. He had gone to bed talking about all the horses he was sure he would get to see the next day, surprising David with all the names of the horses that he remembered.

If David had had any sense he would have waited until that morning to tell his son. Then he would have gotten a good night's sleep. Marking it down as just another lesson learned in the single parent department, he made himself climb out of bed.

There was a slight nervousness in the middle of his stomach as he made breakfast for his son. Was it the excitement of starting something new and spending time around the horses or was it fear of looking a fool in front of Sarah that was making his stomach feel like it was doing summersaults? She made it look so easy when she was up on a horse but with his luck he'd fall off the minute he climbed up on one which would most definitely injure his manly pride along with his backside.

And then there was that strange attraction he felt while watching this new Sarah around the horses, an attraction that shouldn't have been there. They had taken their relationship out of the work environment and with Sarah that felt a little dangerous now. He had no business thinking of Sarah as anything other than a colleague when his life was already full with the new fellowship and taking care of his son. Any kind of relationship other than friendship with Sarah was a complication that he didn't need in his life. His first priority would always be taking care of Davey. Just the time and planning it took to make sure that all his medications were taken on time and all his follow-up appointments were made was a lot more than anyone who hadn't lived with a child with a heart defect would understand. Lisa certainly had never understood.

But wouldn't Sarah?

He picked up the phone to cancel his lesson then looked over to where his son was struggling to get his new cowboy boots on and cancelled the call. He couldn't disappoint Davey. He was reminded of his promise to the little boy when he had lain surrounded by tubes and monitors that the two of them would have a life full of adventure. Even now he had no idea what the future held for his son. He had seen too much already while working with the young transplant patients at the hospital to not know that there was always a chance that Davey could go into rejection or that his new heart could go into heart failure.

He knew all the numbers, the percentages and the years that he could expect for his son to live with his new heart, and he wasn't going to let the two of them miss out on any of the time they had together. Not that he was taking any chances with Davey. He'd already bought a helmet to wear when he was on one of the horses, something that had not made Davey happy as he had insisted that cowboys wore cowboy hats, not helmets. He knew he had made a mistake when he had pulled up a video of a bull rider with a helmet on to show Davey which had set his son into wanting to ride "cows" too.

By the time they had arrived at the horse stables, though, David was sure he had made the right decision. He was taking what was surely just Davey's safety too seriously. Being around the horses had brought more pleasure in his son's life than he'd had in a long time and just watching his son's eyes light up was worth falling off a horse a dozen times. At least that was what he had thought before Sarah had led out a horse much bigger than the one he'd seen the kids riding the last time he had been there.

"It's okay, Daddy, Mr. Jack says Sarah teaches kids all the time."

David looked down to where his son was gently patting his hand, something David had done to him countless times when Davey had been nervous about a procedure, and he smiled down at his son. How had he gotten so lucky to have been given this little boy?

"Come on, Davey. Let's go find someplace where we can watch your daddy," Jack said as he took the boy's hand and they walked out of the stable.

"You do what Mr. Jack tells you, Davey. No running off," David said as he watched them walk away.

"He'll be okay," Sarah said, then turned back to the horse she had brought out for him.

"This is Fancy," Sarah said as she ran her hands over the horse, a movement that seemed to calm the horse. "She's the queen of the farm right now, or at least she thinks so."

"I don't know what makes her a queen, but she is certainly a beautiful horse," David said as he walked up to where Sarah was standing and reached his hand out to touch the stately animal whose coat was solid brown except for her two front feet that were snowy white. Was she what they called a painted horse? He didn't know anything about the different types of horses, something he planned to change by stopping at a bookstore on the way home.

As his hand replaced Sarah's on the horse's neck, Fancy turned her head and looked down at him with a haughty glare that was surely meant to put him in his place.

"I'm not sure she likes me," David said as he slowly removed his hand.

"She's just trying to intimidate you," Sarah said with a laugh. Looking over at her he was once more reminded of how comfortable she appeared here on the farm. It was like she shed her no-nonsense air along with the starched white medical coat she wore at work. Not that she was some stuffed shirt at work. He had been amazed by the way she interacted with the children at the hospital, but here, with the horses, it was like her whole body relaxed. She seemed to have an intimate relationship with each one and he found himself wondering more about her—how she got to be here. Had she always had a love of horses? Or had she married into this family and the horse life?

"Fancy, this is David. He just wants to be your friend," Sarah said as she moved back to the horse and started making some nonsense sounds that seemed to comfort the horse so that the horse stopped giving him the evil eye.

Sarah took David by the hand and then dropped it quickly.

"I'm sorry," Sarah said, a sheepish smile

tugged at her lips. "I'm just so used to working with kids."

"Don't apologize," David said. "Please, teach me just the way you would one of your kids. They probably know more about horses than I do right now."

"Okay, then," she said as she took David's hand and placed it under hers. "Every horse has their own way of wanting to be patted. Your job is to watch how the horse responds.

"Fancy here thinks she's above all that patting and scratching. She likes a smooth rub from here—" she placed his hand on the top of the horse's neck "—to here," she said as she brought both of their hands down the horse's neck to where the saddle sat then moved it back up slowly, then down again. They stood there, close together, for what could have been only a minute with their hands joined together, neither talking as they comforted the horse, the only sound their breathing.

As Sarah removed her hand from his,

David took a deep breath he hadn't known he needed. His body stirred with an arousal that surprised him. He hadn't responded to the touch of a woman's hand in he didn't know how long.

Okay, this was stupid. He'd asked Sarah to teach him as she would any of her other students, but that didn't mean he had to act like some teenage boy with a crush on his pretty teacher. He wasn't an inexperienced kid. He'd learned the hard way that you couldn't let attraction override your brain. His whole relationship with Lisa had been built on physical attraction and look how that had ended. And he had even more to consider now. He had Davey.

"Well, I think you'll be okay with her now," said Sarah as she stepped back away from him. What exactly had just happened between the two of them? Or had it just been him that had felt that spark of attraction?

She handed him a rope she called the leads and he led the horse out into a small fenced area she referred to as a paddock. As Sarah went on to explain all the parts of the saddle and what their uses were, he wished he had made that stop at the bookstore sooner. He'd make a point to take the time to study before his next lesson.

"Now that Fancy is a little more comfortable with you, I think that you should be safe to mount her," Sarah said as she walked back up to the horse and took hold of the lead rope.

"Safe?" he asked as he swallowed down the dread he had felt earlier that morning. He could already picture himself lying on his backside in the dirt with Sarah standing over him.

"You'll be perfectly safe," Sarah said, then gave him a mischievous smile. "I've never lost a student yet."

David put his leg in the stirrup as she had shown him how to do earlier, then with a leap of faith born from the knowledge that Sarah knew what she was doing, he lifted his other leg over the horse.

"Relax, David. Fancy can smell fear a mile away, relax your seat and take the reins," Sarah said as she handed him the leather straps.

As Sarah explained the use of the reins and the other parts of the bridle, both he and Fancy began to relax and by the end of the lesson he had managed to take the two of them in a circular walk around the yard with Fancy protesting only mildly.

"You did great," Sarah said as they led Fancy out to a bigger paddock.

"Are you talking to me or the horse?" he asked. He felt a bit silly about his first reaction to the horse. He'd had a good time learning how to interact with the beautiful animal.

And it hadn't hurt that he'd had a beautiful teacher too.

He thought of the feeling of her hand on his again. No, that didn't mean a thing. It was strictly male appreciation for a lovely woman and no more.

He looked over to where he'd last seen

Davey standing on a small bench outside the paddock and froze.

"Where's Davey?" he asked, not trying to keep the panic out of his voice.

"It's okay. He's with Jack. I saw them walk toward the house. I'm sure they'll be back in just a minute," Sarah said.

He looked down the road where he knew the house had to be. How had Sarah seen Davey leave when he hadn't?

"The lesson isn't over, cowboy, till we put the tack up," Sarah said, trying to get David's attention back to the horse. She knew her father-in-law would never let anything happen to Davey. She hoped that David would know that too. She could see the time away from David was good for Davey and hanging out with Davey was good for Jack too. Not that she could blame David for being so cautious. She was the last person to judge David's parenting. He had been through a lot with Davey and you could see what a wonderful job he was doing with the happy little boy.

Sarah removed the saddle and bridle from Fancy then shut the paddock gate. She watched as the horse headed across the large yard to where a water trough waited for her. Looking over at the man standing beside her, she could see the same look of wonder she'd seen on most of her students after their first lesson. When it came to horses, the beauty and excitement they generated was enough to enchant all ages. Except it hadn't been just David that had been enchanted, for that moment when they had been alone in the stable, their hands touching, their bodies so close, she'd felt as spellbound herself. She'd had to remind herself that she was there to teach David about horses, not flirt with her student. What had gotten into her? This was not how she allowed herself to respond to men. She was a mature widow who had lived without a man in her life for three years now. She had no business responding to one of her colleagues. She'd made sure to keep her distance during the lesson itself, but it still ate at her as David came to stand next to her to watch Fancy as she cantered off to the other side of the fenced yard.

"Let me take that," he said as he reached out for the horse tacking in her hands. As he took the saddle from her she was careful to make sure that she kept her hands away from his, and then she laughed at the ridiculousness of her reactions.

"What?" he asked as he heaved the saddle up on his shoulder as they walked back toward the stable.

"Nothing," she said. She wasn't about to explain how stupid she was acting. She was sure the man had seen more than his quota of women that had fallen all over him. She wasn't going to give him any ideas that she was like those women. Because she wasn't. She had just been being silly about something that she had done with plenty of her students, she just wasn't used to having a man's hands on hers, not anymore at least.

The sight of Jack and Davey coming toward them with her late husband's dog, Pepper, in tow swept away any thoughts she had left of her reaction to David. It was her reaction to Davey that was the problem she needed to concentrate on. Part of her wanted to scoop the little boy up in her arms and hold him close while another part warned her that becoming too involved with the little boy could only lead to heartache when he and his father left Houston after his father's fellowship was complete. And always there was that question in the back of her mind that she found herself wanting to ask. The one question she had no business asking.

Does my son's heart beat in your chest?

Of course she would never ask such a thing of the little boy, she couldn't even come up with a way to approach the subject with David. No, it was best if she just treated this child as the adorable little boy that he was instead of asking herself all of these *what if* questions.

"You two look like you've had fun," she said to Jack and Davey.

"This is Pepper, Daddy, he knows a lot of tricks," Davey said as they all headed back into the stable. "Mr. Jack says it was his son's dog, but his son isn't here anymore because he died and went to heaven."

"I'm very sorry to hear that," David said as he looked over to her and Jack. He rubbed his hand behind his neck and Sarah could see he was worried about her and Jack's feelings with what could be an awkward conversation.

Bending down she petted Pepper. Kolton had gotten the black lab while the two of them had still been in college. Though now more gray than black, the dog was still up for a game of fetch when she had the time.

"I'm sure Kolton would be happy to know a little boy like you was playing with Pepper," she said to Davey then gave the dog a last scratch behind its ear.

"That's what Mr. Jack said," Davey said as he took up the petting of the dog.

"Davey, would you like to help me put some of this tack up?" She held out her arms and showed him the equipment she was carrying. "Jack, can you show David what to do with that saddle?"

As they put away Fancy's equipment, Sarah listened to the little boy talk about the time he had spent with "Mr. Jack." It was plain to see that Davey was enjoying the time he had spent on the farm and she was reminded of all those dreams she and Kolton had for their own son when they'd watched him running around the grounds of the farm. They'd planned to fill their house with children and had looked forward to sharing their love of horses with them. But those dreams had ended in just one second by a driver trying to make it through a yellow light. There wouldn't be children filling her home or running around the farm now. That dream had died with her family. There would be no more children for Sarah. Even if she met a man she wanted to have a relationship with it would never be the same as she had with Kolton. And she would never risk having children again. She wouldn't be able to live with the knowledge that she could lose them at any second. She wasn't even sure what Jack would do with the farm once he was too old to keep it up.

"And then Mr. Jack showed me all the trophies his son had won in the rodeo and he said some of them were yours, too," Davey said as he turned toward her. Sarah blinked. She hadn't thought about those old trophies in years.

"What is that?" David asked as he and Jack joined them again. "You've won trophies?"

"She was a champion barrel racer," Jack said, smiling over at her with pride. "You've never seen anything like the way she could get her horse to respond to her."

"Really? I had no idea you had so many hidden talents," David teased as he looked back over to her.

"It was many years ago." Heat flooded her face, "I haven't raced since I finished college."

Her days of racing were long gone but after Kolton and Cody's death, she had discovered the only place she felt like she was in control was on the back of her horse, far away from people where she could cry and scream and not have to worry about what other people thought of her.

By the time David and Davey had left the farm, Sarah was ready for a good long ride. The tension of being around the little boy and the pain and joy that it brought to see him enjoying himself around the horses had confused her. The thought of all her son would miss made her heart raw with emotion. But Davey's laughter was like a bandage to her soul.

When she and Sugar made it to the back

pasture, she let the horse run. It wasn't until they topped the hill that she realized where she had come. Looking down across the field she saw the large white stone and mortar house with its covered windows and locked doors. Hers and Kolton's forever house where they had planned to raise Cody and later his brothers and sisters. Only now her forever family was gone and her dream home was as empty and lonely as she was herself.

She dismounted the horse and sat down on the green grass. There should have been good memories there, memories of all the firsts they had experienced: Cody's first words, first steps and the first night she and Kolton had spent the night making love in that big king size bed that he had insisted they buy. Had she let the pain of their loss steal all the good memories away from her?

The field was full of the new growth of spring. The flowers around the front entrance that she had planted with Kolton would be starting to peak their heads out of their winter beds by now. Soon there would be scarlet sage and hummingbird mint filling the garden. They'd picked the white stone of the house so that the flowers would be showcased against the stark color. They'd spent hours planning everything in the house. It was the only one they'd ever planned to build and they hadn't wanted to have any regrets.

But now she did have regrets. Her life was full of them and she instinctively knew that if she didn't share with David her suspicions as far as her son and his son were concerned that she would just be adding more regrets to her life. She didn't want that for her or for David. She had to find a way to tell him before it was too late.

Sarah stopped in front of Breanna's hospital room door. Inside she could hear someone crying. There were a lot of tears shared on the pediatric cardiac floor, some were happy, but there were a lot of sad tears too. While Sarah wanted to give her patient's family their privacy, she had to see if there was anything she could do to help. She knocked on the door and entered to find the young mother she had met only the week before in a rocking chair crying while her little girl slept surrounded by tubes and machines. Maggie looked up at Sarah as she entered, her face streaked with tears that she was too tired to wipe away. Sarah had once been a young mother all alone waiting at the bedside of her child waiting to see if her son was going to wake up, too tired to hide the sight of her tears from others.

"Hey, Maggie, I just wanted to check on you. Is there anything I can do to help?" Sarah said. "I know all of this is very scary, but I've spoken with the cardiologist and the cardiac surgeon and they say Breanna's doing really well after her surgery."

Maggie looked from her child to Sarah.

"I know she's better. She's so pink now, just like a normal baby, but she isn't normal. She's hooked up to all those tubes and I can't even hold her except when the nurses are there to help. I don't even think she knows who I am," Maggie said as she started to cry again. "And I know I should be happy that she's doing so much better, but I just can't help it. It wasn't supposed to be like this. John worked so hard on the nursery and we haven't even been home since I went into labor. And now John's left because he has to go back to work."

Sarah moved over to a chair beside Maggie where she sat hugging herself then wrapped her arms around the young woman. She didn't have the answer to all of Maggie's worries right now, but she could at least give her some company.

"I know it's hard going through all of this, especially now that John is gone, but we are here to help."

"I know," Maggie said as she grabbed a tissue from a half-empty box. "Everyone's been great. It's just I never dreamed this would happen, you know? You always hear of things like this happening to other people, but you never think it could happen to you."

Sarah felt her heart squeeze for a moment. She knew only too well how it felt when you realize that the horrendous things that happen to other people have happened to you.

"How about we move the rocking chair over to the crib and I'll help you hold Breanna?"

Sarah left the room after sharing her number and the number of another mother who lived in the Houston area whose child had been born with the same congenital defect as Breanna and who was happy to help with other families. Maggie had promised she would call one of them if she needed to talk, but Sarah would check back with her before she left for the day. It was hard for some people to reach out to others as she well knew.

Speaking with Breanna's nurse, she shared that she had helped Maggie get Breanna from the crib and the two of them were doing fine though the nurse would need to check on them shortly.

Sarah turned to see David talking to another nurse, before he waved at her and headed her way.

"What's up?" she asked as he joined her on the way out of the unit.

"I saw you come out of little Breanna's room. Is everything okay?" he asked.

"Breanna's doing great. It's her mother that's a mess right now. Her husband, John, had to leave to return to work and she's all alone. Add to that the fears of any new mother and it's just a lot. She's really worried about losing the bonding time that most mothers get with their baby. I think we just need to work harder to get her involved with Breanna's care."

The overhead speaker squawked then a

monotone voice started to speak. "Code blue, PCIC room ten."

As the speaker repeated the information, the two of them ran back down the hall.

"It's Lindsey," she said to David as they pushed past the rest of the staff. As the charge nurse assigned jobs, she rushed over to the nurse performing compressions on the small chest.

"What happened?" David asked as he moved behind the bed with the respiratory tech and prepared to intubate.

"She suddenly desated down to the sixties. By the time I got in here she was in PEA," the nurse said as one of the patient techs took over the compressions.

"Have you given her any meds?" David asked as he expertly inserted the endotracheal tube with a skill that she would have expected from an older, more experienced doctor.

"Giving epinephrine now," said Mel as she pushed the medication into an IV line.

David moved back and the respiratory tech quickly hooked up the Ambu bag to the ET tube and started squeezing the bag that would force the air into her lungs. Sarah watched as Lindsey's chest began to rise up and down. Checking the monitors she could see that the oxygen saturation was rising.

"It's time for a rhythm check," the charge nurse called out. The room turned silent as they all turned to look at the monitor.

"See if we have a pulse with that," David said as he checked the carotid and Sarah checked the femoral. She held her breath.

Please let them get this sweet girl back.

Then she felt the weak beat under her fingers that told her that Lindsey was back with them again.

"We have a pulse," David announced to the room. It was as if the room itself let out a deep sigh, then the world returned to normal with everyone talking at once.

Sarah moved with David to check the monitor.

"She's still not oxygenating well," David said.

"She was doing so much better before this respiratory infection. Her heart's just not strong enough to handle the extra work," Sarah said as she started looking through her phone for Lindsey's mother's number.

"Dr. Benton is in the OR. I'm going to call into the room and talk to him. She's a perfect candidate for ECMO," David said as she looked over to where Lindsey lay.

Gone was the laughing little girl who had excitedly shown her the pretty unicorn. Now hooked to even more monitors and drips to keep her sedated she lay still and quiet. Too quiet. Lindsey had always been a fighter, but now it was up to Sarah and the staff to fight for her.

"You go talk to Dr. Benton. I'm going to call her mother," she said.

"She should've been here. Doesn't she

realize how sick her child is? We'll need her to consent to take Lindsey into the OR."

"She's probably at work. I have the number. I'll get her here even if I have to go get her myself," Sarah said as she started going through the contacts on her phone.

"If she can't do any better than this, how is she going to do when her daughter gets a transplant?" David said angrily before he walked out of the room.

As Sarah began to go through the numbers she had listed for Lindsey's mother, she wondered why David, who was usually so patient with his patients' parents, seemed to have none for the single mom. Sarah knew that David was just concerned about Lindsey, but he had to understand that Hannah, like Breanna's father, had to go to work to make a living to support both herself and her daughter. Although Sarah had to admit that it seemed that Hannah had been spending less time than usual with Lindsey. There was definitely something going on with Hannah and she planned to find out what it was before things went any further. If the mother needed their help she wanted to know. No one should have to go it alone in a situation like this. Only David himself had once done just that.

CHAPTER FOUR

SARAH STAYED IN the waiting room with Hannah while Dr. Benton and David took Lindsey back to the operating room to insert the needed catheters to start the child on the ECMO system that would help her heart and lungs rest while she recovered from the respiratory infection that was making her already failing heart work harder than it could.

The doctors had explained to Hannah that Lindsey had stopped breathing, causing her heart to quit pumping, and that even though they had gotten her heart beating again they couldn't promise that she wouldn't arrest again and that this was the best hope she had to recover.

Now they both waited together, a young mother who was barely holding it together and Sarah who had let her heart become involved with another child who she could lose. Sarah cared for all the children that she took care of in the hospital, but Lindsey was special. The girl had a passion for life and had fought her way through every trial her failing heart had given her. Sarah had shared her love of horses with Lindsey and hadn't been surprised to find that the girl had quickly made friends of all the horses in the stable, which reminded her of another child, a little dark-haired boy who was quickly becoming a favorite around the stable and finding a way into her heart.

For years she had protected her heart from the pain of losing another child she loved and now she sat here knowing that she was dangerously close to knowing that pain again. Only neither child belonged to her. She had to remember that. Right now what she needed to be doing was helping Lindsey's mother as much as possible.

"Hannah, is there anyone you want me

to call?" she asked. As far as Sarah could remember there had never been anyone except for Hannah visiting Lindsey.

"No, thank you," Hannah said as she pulled at the cuffs of her sleeves.

"Are you cold? I can get you a warm blanket. These waiting rooms are always too cold," Sarah offered, then looked back over at the young woman who stared at the entrance to the waiting room as if in a trance. Reaching for Hannah's hand she squeezed it.

"It's okay, Hannah. You're not alone," Sarah said as they sat there with their hands joined as they waited for news of Lindsey's condition.

Moments later David and a very tired-looking Dr. Benton came into the waiting room.

"She made it through," Dr. Benton said, taking a seat next to Hannah.

Sarah stood and left as Dr. Benton explained the plan they had for Lindsey's care to her mother.

"I know that this was the best thing for Lindsey right now, but do you think her heart will be strong enough after she gets over this respiratory issue to come off the machine?" she asked David.

David rubbed the back of his neck, something that she was beginning to notice he did often when he was worried which didn't make her feel any better about Lindsey's chances.

"To be honest, I don't know. We discussed it before we spoke with Hannah and we all agreed that it was the only choice we had right now. If her lungs get better she'll have a much better chance. Dr. Benton's going to see about getting her moved up on the transplant list as soon as she starts turning around. Till then, we let her rest and we hit her with everything we have to wipe out this infection," said David as he rubbed the back of his neck again. "I wish I knew something else to do, but for now we just have to wait."

It seemed to Sarah that Lindsey had

been waiting most of her life for a chance to live a normal existence, instead of one that was spent having one medical procedure after another, being in and out of the hospital, and never getting to be the little girl that she deserved a chance to be. Sarah knew life didn't always work the way it was planned. Her own life was proof of that, but she had to believe that Lindsey would someday have the life that she deserved. She just needed to hang in there until a heart could be found for her. Until then all they could do was wait.

Sarah watched as David once again tangled the reins as he tried to apply the bridle. She held back a laugh when Fancy turned and gave him one of her haughty looks that plainly said she wasn't impressed. David had arrived with a new air of confidence until Sarah had told him that he would be tacking his own horse that day. It might have been that distraction that had made him agree for Jack to take Davey up to the house to see one of the smaller ponies; though it hadn't been enough for him to not insist that they come back as soon as they finished. She had expected her father-in-law to balk at that instruction, but Jack seemed to understand that David wasn't trying to be rude. He just felt the need to watch over his son a little more than the normal parent.

"It looked so easy in the book. I don't understand what I'm doing wrong," he said as he let go of the tangled reins and moved away from the horse.

Jumping down from the gate she had been sitting on, Sarah reached out and took the bridle from him and once more showed him how to make sure that it didn't tangle with the other straps. Taking pity on all three of them, she finished putting on the bridle. With the bit safely in Fancy's mouth, she handed the reins to David and mounted Sugar.

"Come on, let's go have some fun," Sarah said as she made a clicking sound with her tongue and started across to where she'd opened the gate to a large pasture. After a minute of a very one-sided conversation, Fancy decided she'd let David follow behind Sarah.

"Remember feet all the way in the stirrup, turned in like you're hugging Fancy with your legs," she said as she rode up to him then reached over and placed her hands on his lower back and abdomen.

"Shoulders back and back straight," she said as felt his abdomen tighten under her hand. She ran her other hand up his back to his shoulders.

"There. That's perfect," she said, then cleared her throat as she moved her hands away from him. Why did this have to be so awkward? She was just trying to teach him the correct way to sit. There was no reason for it to feel so intimate every time they touched. She whipped Sugar around so that he couldn't see her face and waited for him and Fancy to catch up with her.

For a minute there was only silence between the two of them.

"This is beautiful," he said as they reached the end of the pasture then turned around to face the stretch of green they had just ridden across and the white stables beyond that. "You must love living here."

There had been a time when the answer to that would have come easily. She had grown up not far south of Houston on a much smaller farm where her father and brother raised cattle, so she'd felt right at home after she had married Kolton and they'd moved to the farm to live with Jack. It had been a busy time in their life with Kolton starting his first job after he had graduated with an architect degree and her starting her first job as a nurse. They'd both come home exhausted but excited about their new lives together. They'd been married a year when Jack had given them the land to build their own home, declaring that the house was just too small for the three of them though they both had known Jack was trying to push them out the door so that they could start a family.

After Kolton and Cody were gone she'd known that she could never live in the house that had been so full of promises. She'd planned to move back to the city until Jack had invited her to move back in with him. She couldn't have said no to the man who she had come to love as a second father who was hurting as much as she was.

"It is beautiful," she said, thinking of the house that lay just over the next hill.

"I'm sorry. I didn't think," David said as he began rubbing a hand down Fancy's neck. "You lived here with your husband and son?"

"Yes," she said as she climbed down and looked back away from the pasture to where the woods hid the home the three of them had shared. "We made a life here together. It was all we ever wanted. Kolton was just as horse crazy as I am and we couldn't think of a better place to raise our family. But that part of my life is gone now."

David dismounted, being careful to hold Fancy's reins as Sarah had taught him so that he could still control her. He could tell that Sarah needed to talk to someone about the loss she'd suffered. She was still holding so much pain inside of her that it couldn't be good for her.

"I don't talk about my ex-wife or my divorce either. Not that I'm comparing the two. But sometimes I do wish I could talk about it. It's like by keeping it inside I don't have to deal with it, but I know that's not healthy," he said as they both started walking across the field.

"You can talk to me," Sarah said as she looked over at him, "if you want to, that is."

Surprisingly, he found that he did want to talk to her. If anyone would understand the stress a new baby—a sick new baby—

could put on a marriage, she could. She dealt with not only the young patients they saw, but also their parents.

"When Davey was born with a heart defect we didn't know what to expect. By the time he was two he'd had four surgeries. He went on the transplant waiting list after the last one."

"A lot of marriages have trouble when they have a chronically sick child. You know that," said Sarah. "Did your wife have any medical experience?"

The only thing Lisa had experience with had been manipulating men, though he hadn't known that until it was too late. The woman had made a fool of him long before Davey had been born. He could have forgiven her that, but he would never forgive her for running out on their son when he had needed them the most. A part of him had known from the beginning Lisa didn't have it in her to accept what life with Davey would mean, but he had hoped that for the sake of his son that she would be able to change.

"No. Lisa blamed a lot of her problems with dealing with Davey on the fact that he was always sick. She even blamed the time he spent in the hospital for the reason she hadn't bonded with him." He remembered the anger he had felt at that remark.

"She finally decided that she didn't have the time for a sick child like Davey in her life and then she was gone. Davey seldom mentions his mother, but then why would he when he hasn't seen her since his second birthday when she had arrived expecting a birthday party to only find Davey back in the hospital." And instead of staying with their son till he was well enough to leave the hospital she'd laid a fancy wrapped present on the bed and left.

"Are you afraid that she'll come back one day and want to be part of Davey's life?" Sarah asked.

She unexpectedly reached for his hand then squeezed it. When she began to pull it away, he held it tighter. He had started this conversation to help Sarah be able to talk to him, to help her deal with the pain that he suspected was holding her back from moving on with her life, but here she was helping him instead. Holding her warm hand in his seemed to ease the pain and anger that he felt whenever he talked about his ex-wife.

"A part of me is afraid she'll come back and another part of me is afraid that she won't. Davey deserves to have a mother in his life." Right now all he knew was having a father, but someday that little boy would ask him why his mother wasn't there and he didn't know what he'd say to him.

As they neared the paddock, David was surprised to see his son sitting on top of a squat pony being led by Jack. He dropped Sarah's hand before they got closer. It wouldn't do for either Jack or Davey to get the wrong idea about their relationship.

"Daddy, look at me," Davey said as they got closer. "Look Miss Sarah, I'm riding just like my daddy."

"I see," Sarah said as they both stopped.

"The boy's a natural and Humphrey needed some exercise. I hope you don't mind," Jack said.

David started to assure the older man that he didn't have a problem with Davey on the pony when he realized that Jack hadn't been talking to him. It was Sarah that he'd wanted to make sure was okay that Davey was riding. Did her father-in-law think that Sarah didn't trust him with Davey? But that didn't make any sense at all.

"It's fine, Jack. Humphrey is perfect for Davey right now," she said, then turned away and went inside the building.

Then it hit him. Humphrey must have been her son's horse. How old had the child been? The pony was a good fit for Davey partly because he was much smaller than most of the children his age. Had her son been younger? There were so many questions he had and none of them were his business he reminded himself.

"He was your son's pony? I'll understand if you don't want Davey on him, again," he assured her, though right now he wasn't sure how he would be able to talk his son off the pony.

"It's fine," she said as she looked back over at him. "I mean it. Let's get this tack up and I'll show you the proper way to brush out a horse." A small smile crossed her lips, but it didn't reach her eyes.

They worked in silence till they were joined by Davey and Jack.

"That was the best!" said Davey as he led the small pony inside with Jack walking beside him. "And Mr. Jack says I can take him back to the house and tackle him."

"I think he meant that you could put up his tack— that's the saddle and reins, like me and your dad are doing here," Sarah said as the three adults laughed at his son's

expression. This time he was relieved to
see that her smile touched her eyes.

"Okay. He said I could do that tack thing
and then we're going to eat some beans
like the cowboys used to do," Davey said,
then smiled at Jack. David had never gotten that reaction from his son when he'd
tried to get him to eat his beans.

"I said we'd have to ask your dad,
Davey," Jack said as he rubbed the top of
Davey's head affectionately.

"Ah…" David looked at Sarah, obvi-
ously not sure how she would feel having
the two of them suddenly to dinner.

"That sounds like an excellent plan,"
she said as she took the pony's lead in
one hand and his son's hand in the other
and started down the road that led to the
house.

That night Sarah was unable to sleep,
struggling with the knowledge that she
hadn't taken her chance to tell David about
her suspicions. That Davey had been given

her son's donated heart the night she had seen him in the waiting room. She'd had the perfect moment when they had been alone on the horses, but then David had brought up the subject of his ex-wife and she couldn't deny that she was curious about what had happened between the two of them. Once again, he had shared more of himself than she had. It only made the guilt of keeping everything from him worse.

When Jack had invited the two back to the house for dinner, she had felt herself being drawn in even more by the charming little boy. And then there had been the question that always ate at her when she was around the little boy.

Does some part of my Cody still live on in you?

She found herself wanting to hug the little boy to her and to rest her head on his chest just to listen to the beating of his heart.

She knew she should have come clean

with David the first time she had met him and realized who he was.

But she hadn't been ready to deal with the possibility herself. Only now that she had waited till she was ready, she was afraid that David would be angry with her for not sharing this earlier.

She'd finally fallen asleep after she had come to the decision to share what she knew with David as soon as possible and let him decide if he wanted to learn the truth. Only when she awoke the old doubts were back. What if David didn't want to know his son's donor family? There was a reason why Organ Procurement didn't allow them to communicate unless both parties were in agreement. And what if he decided not to bring Davey to the ranch anymore? She hadn't seen Jack enjoy himself as much as he did with Davey after his son and grandson had been killed, and Jack didn't even know yet about the circumstances of Davey's heart transplant.

Arriving at the hospital early, she wanted

to spend some time with Lindsey before she started her regular rounds. She'd gotten a message from the cardiopulmonary perfusionist that they had decreased the sedation that morning and that Lindsey was responsive. Entering the room, she was overwhelmed by the amount of machinery that was keeping such a little girl alive. A cacophony of beeps, clicks and occasionally a high-pitched alarm greeted her. In among all the machines she was surprised to see Hannah sitting in a small chair at the side of the bed asleep with her head resting next to her daughter. Trying not to wake her, Sarah spoke quietly to one of the nurses that was assigned to keep all the machines working properly as another nurse continually monitored Lindsey.

"How is she?" she asked Jose, who sat the farthest away from the sleeping mom.

"She's holding on. She got too anxious when she saw her mom so we had to increase the sedation again," he said.

Sarah left the room and headed for the doctors' workroom where hopefully someone had started a large pot of coffee. She'd need the caffeine. Sleepless nights were not something that she could afford to have when she was dealing with critically ill patients and their families. The doctors she worked with depended on her to keep her eyes and ears open for anything that could go wrong with their patients and right then her eyes were not cooperating.

She'd finished her second cup and had reviewed several of her patients' new lab work by the time David and Dr. Benton showed up.

"We just left Lindsey," David said as he poured himself a cup.

"I just checked this morning's X-rays and there is some improvement," she said as she pulled them up on her computer. David bent over her as they both reviewed the newest film that showed a small amount of improvement in her lungs. As he reached around her to point at a whited-out part on her right lung, Sarah found herself tensing as the warm heat of his body surrounded her.

At once she was overcome with a desire to curl up inside the arms that encased her. The need to be held and loved filled her body making it difficult to breathe, to think. Surprised by the deep longing that almost had her turning into David's arms, she pushed away from the desk forcing him to step back away from her.

What was wrong with her? It wasn't like the man had been making a pass at her. Thankfully he hadn't seemed to notice her reaction to his closeness. It had to be the guilt of holding back the information about her son that was making her feel so uncomfortable around him. That was it. All she had to do was have a conversation with him and all these uncomfortable feelings would go away.

"David, if you have a minute—" she looked over to where Dr. Benton was working on his own computer "—I need to talk to you."

"We've got a few minutes before we head back to surgery," he said as he took the seat beside her. "What's wrong? Is there something else about Lindsey?"

"No, it doesn't have anything to do with work. It's something else I need to tell you," she looked back over at Dr. Benton hoping that he would take the hint that she didn't want to talk in front of the other MD. David's eyes followed hers and then he seemed to understand.

"If it's about Davey and the pony, you don't need to worry about it. You know how children are, he'll have forgotten about him in a day or two. Next time we're at the ranch he'll fall in love with another animal," he said. "Actually I wanted to talk to you. Dr. Benton has offered to let me take his place at the UNOS conference in Dallas this weekend so I'm going to have to cancel my next lesson."

David was going to the conference instead of Dr. Benton? That meant that they'd be there together. "I'd meant to cancel the lesson myself as I'm going to be out of town at the conference too."

"I'm sorry, Sarah," Dr. Benton said from behind her. "I meant to tell you I was going to have to cancel. The wife is insistent that I stay in town till the next grandchild is born, though between the three of us I'd much rather be at the conference. I hate all that waiting in the waiting rooms. It seemed a shame to waste the registration fee and it's a great chance for David to meet some of the board members."

"What about Davey?" she asked. She was torn between hoping that she would finally have a good opportunity to talk to David about her son and concerned about being alone with the man after the way her body had just reacted to his.

"His nanny has agreed to stay over. Ms. Duggar's a retired nurse and is great with him. I'll have all his medications ready for her with a timer set and I can be back in an hour by plane if I need to be," David said as he raised one of his hands toward the back of his neck.

"I'm sure he'll be fine," she said. It had to be hard to leave his son alone in a new city, especially after all that Davey had been through and how protective he was of his son. Though she should probably do Ms. Duggar a favor and have a talk with David, she knew by watching him with Davey and Jack at the ranch that he could be a little overprotective.

"So it's settled," Dr. Benton said as he started back toward the door. "It's a very informative conference and the two of you will have a great time."

"Oh, wait," David said. "You said you wanted to talk to me. What's up?"

"It's nothing that can't wait till later," she said. It had waited this long, after all.

"How about we share a ride? I know you had been planning on riding with Dr. Benton to Dallas. We can talk then," David said.

"Sure," she said, then watched as the two men headed back to the surgical department. For the first time that day she felt as if she was free to relax. She'd been given a reprieve from having to come clean with David, at least for a few days. She would clear the air between them. She'd come clean about the night that she had seen him in the waiting room and her son's donation. By the time they returned from Dallas everything would be settled as far as whether they wanted to find out about their donor and recipient relationship or not and she'd be able to move on from there. There would be no more of these pangs of guilt or the butterflies when she was around David. They would be able to return to the comfortable friendship that they had enjoyed earlier.

CHAPTER FIVE

BY THE TIME the two of them had set out for Dallas, David and Sarah both had put in a full day at the hospital. Lindsey had improved to the point that some of the sedation was being weaned down and her lungs had improved enough that Dr. Benton had called a meeting of the whole transplant team from the social worker to the cardiologist so that they could all work together to make a case on why Lindsey needed to be moved to the top of the transplant list at this time.

It had fascinated him to see all the parts of the team work together. It reminded him that it had once been his son's case that had been discussed at length while he waited for the outcome. What if they hadn't agreed to ask to move Davey up on the transplant list? It had been a miracle that a heart had become available when it did.

"He'll be okay," Sarah said from the passenger seat next to him.

"It shows, huh?" David said as he rubbed at the back of his neck.

"A bit," she said with a mysterious laugh.

"What's so funny?" he asked. Did she find the fact that he was worried about his son funny? He sure didn't think so. "It's the first time we've been separated like this."

He opened his mouth to say something about her not understanding, and then stopped. He had no idea what had happened to her son and husband. If he had learned anything in the few years that he had worked in the medical field, he had learned to appreciate the fact that there was always someone out there who was going through more than you. He had no right to assume that his path with his son had been harder than the path she had taken with hers. He still had Davey but her son was lost to her forever.

"You don't realize, do you?" she asked.

"Okay, tell me. What is it?" he asked. He couldn't help but smile at the playfulness in her voice.

"I don't think I should," she said. "It would just make it worse if you knew you were doing it."

"Doing what?" he asked. He wasn't doing anything except driving. He looked over at Sarah where she sat curled up in the seat next to him looking more relaxed than she had all week.

"It's just that you have this telling sign when you're worried. Hasn't anyone ever told you?" she asked.

What was she talking about? He looked back from the road to her. "You're kidding right?" he asked as he returned his eyes to the road. Traffic on I-45 was beginning to get heavy.

"No. I can't believe no one's ever told you. I would have thought at least your wife—I mean ex-wife—would have mentioned it," she said.

"Lisa? She had a tendency to be more wrapped up in herself," he said.

"I'm curious. Where did you meet her?"

"I met Lisa in medical school at Tulane, a year before I was supposed to graduate," he said. He rubbed the back of his neck again then turned toward Sarah to see her lips curve up into a smile. What was with the woman today?

"But you said she wasn't clinical," Sarah said.

"She was an art history major, with a couple minors I can't remember now, but no she didn't want anything to do with the medical field," he said. "She was smart and pretty and before I knew it was happening we were moving in together."

He remembered that first day when they'd moved into one of the small shotgun houses in the not-quite-respectable part of New Orleans. While not happy with the location, Lisa had been thrilled with the architectural details of the old house.

"It wasn't till later that I realized I had given Lisa the wrong idea about my situation." He'd never dreamed that she had assumed that he had a well-off family bankrolling him through college just because he drove a vintage sports car that he and his dad had fixed up. "It's silly really. I should have seen the signs, but I guess no one wants to think that someone is only interested in their bank account. By the time she figured out that the only thing I was going to have when I finished school was several hundred thousand dollars of tuition debt, she was pregnant with Davey."

"I'm sorry. You must have felt hurt," Sarah said.

The sun had begun to set and the shadows were beginning to fill the car as they drove in silence for a few minutes.

"I don't remember to be honest. I was so busy with school and getting my residency set up that I really didn't have the time to feel much of anything. By the time Davey was born I was deep in my last year of medical school." His whole life had revolved around his education until Davey.

"By the time we discovered that something was wrong with Davey, our marriage was already a mess. Lisa made it clear from the beginning that she wasn't willing to wait around until I got established to have all the things she wanted. She had a certain lifestyle planned for herself and I don't think me and Davey had a place in it. I came home one day to find her packing, with a woman I had never met in the house taking care of Davey. He'd had his first operation by then and we had him on a strict schedule with his medication. I couldn't believe that she was just going to leave him. I mean what kind of mother does that?" He didn't give Sarah a chance to respond. What was there really for her to say that he hadn't already said himself?

"It seemed that while our son was recovering from cardiac surgery, his mother had been job hunting via the internet and had taken up an online relationship with a very well-off art gallery owner. So while I'd been at work, thinking that she was taking care of our son, she'd been planning a new life with a French guy named Marchard. He had the status and money that Lisa wanted and that was all that was important to her. A month later the divorce papers showed up. She didn't even file for visitation rights with Davey."

The car was quiet when he finished. Filled with his anger for the way Lisa had treated their son. It had been years since she had left them. How long was he going to let it affect him?

"I don't want you to think that I resent raising Davey by myself," he said. "I don't."

"I'd never think that. The way you've managed to care for Davey is amazing. It's plain to see how much you love that little boy," Sarah said. "What will you do if she comes back and wants Davey?" asked Sarah.

"I'll never let that happen. I promised Davey when he was waiting for a heart that it would always be just the two of us together. I'd never let someone break us up."

He had done all the talking and now Sarah knew all of his past. Maybe she would be ready to share some of her past with him. "What about you? Where did you meet your husband?" he asked.

"The rodeo community isn't as large as you would think. It seems as if we had known each other forever. We started dating in high school and were married before we graduated from college," she said. Only the interior lights lit the car now, but he could see that she hadn't turned away from him as she had at other times when she'd discussed her family.

"So it was a good marriage?" he asked,

surprised by the small tinge of jealousy that filled him.

"It was a very good marriage," she said. "We both had goals for our careers and of course we both loved horses. By the time we were married we had become best friends."

"I'm glad. I know you didn't have a lot of time together, but at least it was good." He knew he had gone too far when she moved farther to the other side of her seat and then she surprised him.

"Would you ever consider getting married again?" she asked.

"I don't know. I really don't think much about it. Right now my first priority is Davey. I have to put him before everything. What about you?"

"No," Sarah answered as they arrived at the convention hotel. Somehow the answer didn't surprise him. Sarah was willing to give everything of herself to the people she cared for but it seemed to him that she didn't ask much for herself.

"Don't think that I've forgotten that you still haven't answered my question about what this *telling* sign I have is when I'm worried," he said, changing the subject, as he opened his car door.

As the valet opened the door for Sarah, she reached over and rubbed her hand up the back of his neck, the motion taking his breath away as she moved even closer, till all he could see was the smile on her all too kissable lips.

"This," she said, then climbed out of the car to help with the luggage that the bellboy had begun unpacking.

David reached his hand to the back of his head where she had touched him, then pulled it back. What did you know, the woman was right, he did have a telling sign when he was nervous. And being this close to Sarah was making him very nervous.

David was trying to listen to what Sarah was saying, but he kept being drawn back to the flickering light of the candles as it reflected off her deep brown eyes. Her touch the night before had caused something in him to go haywire. When he should have been taking in all the information in the seminars today, his mind had continually wandered back to that touch, that smile that had lit something inside him, which he was having a problem understanding. Now he sat here like a wide-eyed sap.

His only consolation was that Sarah didn't seemed to have noticed. He knew she had no idea how beautiful she looked tonight dressed in a violet dress with her hair left down to fall past her shoulders. She wasn't a classic beauty like Lisa. No, Sarah's beauty was deeper. It was those deep brown eyes that lit up when she talked about the kids at the hospital or the horses at the farm. Her smile was infectious and the compassion she showed for the parents she dealt with showed him that she was as beautiful on the inside as she was on the outside.

They'd both been required to dress up tonight as one of the organ procurement vendors was hosting a special dinner for the attendees and now that all the ceremonies for the night were finally over and the others from their table had left to mingle, the two of them were alone. Leaving a sense of intimacy that reminded him of the time they'd shared in the dark car driving into Dallas.

But there was something different tonight. Whether it was the atmosphere or just the change their relationship seemed to be going through, he didn't know, but he was becoming more aware of Sarah as a woman then as a co-worker, a very attractive woman who had his body reacting in ways that it hadn't in years.

"What about you?" she asked as she finished informing him about the last seminar she had attended that afternoon, a talk by a group of doctors that were involved in a new research program that hoped to help them determine which chemotherapy drug was the right medicine for their patients' specific cancer. He should have found it fascinating. He did find it fascinating; he just found this woman in the short violet dress more fascinating.

"David?" she asked again as she reached over and took his hand. "Are you okay?"

He looked down to where her hand lay over his. This intimate touch should have bothered him as he wasn't one of those touchy-feely people, but it didn't. Something had changed between the two of them in the past weeks. That was the only way he could explain why he would have bared all the unpleasantness of his marriage, of the hurt he had felt of not being enough, of him and Davey not being enough for the wife who had carelessly left the two of them.

"Why don't you call and check on him?" she asked as she moved her face close to his trying to get his attention. It was the closeness of her lips that brought him to his senses.

"Call who?" he asked, then realized there was only one person that he needed to check on. "I called before he ate his supper to make sure his medicine was given on time. I'm going to call back at bedtime. I've set an alarm."

"So, what do you think of the conference? What did you find out at that statistics seminar as far as this year's numbers?" she asked as she pulled her hand away from his.

"Basically what we all know. The need is great and though the numbers of donations have been rising, there's still a shortage," he said. "I did run into someone from our local procurement office, I think her name is Heather."

"Yes, Heather Long. She's great isn't she," Sarah said as she looked out over the room at the other attendees as if to locate the woman.

"She seems to be. We had a moment to

discuss some of the patients we have listed right now and she seemed to think that we should be able to get Lindsey moved up once she stabilizes. Not that it will make much of a difference if we don't get a donation match soon," he said, then glanced back down at his watch. "What are your plans for tomorrow?"

"I'm attending the forum on donor and recipient relationships and privacy," she said, as once more she looked away from him and scanned the other people in the room. "I'm really looking forward to it. Do you want to go with me?" she asked though she still seemed to be looking over his shoulder.

He glanced back over his shoulder and wondered what it was now that had *her* preoccupied, then turned back to see her eyes had now returned to him. Was she feeling that same strange sense that something was changing between the two of them? Was that what seemed to be making her uncomfortable now?

"I promised Heather I'd attend her talk on how to create a closer community relationship between the local hospitals and the organ procurement programs," he said.

"Oh, okay," she said. He could tell she was disappointed, though he wasn't sure why.

"I thought maybe you'd be interested. You know, because of Davey," she said. She was back to looking past him again. "Do you ever wonder about the donor?"

"I do, sometimes. It's strange. I mean at first I was really busy taking care of Davey, but it was still there in the back of my mind. It's almost like a survivor's guilt. You know when you get a transplant of any kind, unless it's a living transplant of course, that someone lost someone that they loved very much and because of their loss, now someone that you love very much has a chance at life." Just talking about receiving the gift of donation, the gift of another one's child, tore at his heart. How had Sarah managed to live through losing her son as well as her husband?

"I remember one of those first nights after Davey's transplant I was just watching him sleep, just watching how much more comfortable he breathed and marveling at how fast his pale gray cheeks had turned a healthy pink after his surgery. It must have been about two or three days post-op and I couldn't help wondering if somewhere there was another family standing over a casket where their child now lay," he said. He looked up and saw the color blanch from Sarah's face.

"I'm sorry. I know that must sound a bit morbid," he said, relieved when he saw that the color was returning to her face.

"No. I appreciate you sharing that with me," she said, though he noticed the excitement she had shown for the next day seemed to have faded. "Have you ever thought of contacting them?"

He thought for a minute about those first few days and of the guilt he had felt. Had he ever considered contacting his son's donor's family? "No, I guess I always figured that if the donor wanted to contact me I would hear from them. I wouldn't want to cause them any more pain. I really haven't given it as much thought as I should have, I guess."

"Maybe they thought the same way you did," she said her voice a soft whisper across the table.

His phone beeped an alarm and after giving Sarah an apologetic shrug, he made his evening call to Davey. As always his son's happy voice made him feel better and calmed the fears that he always suffered from when he was away from his son. He could be accused of not thinking anyone could care for his son as well as he could and he wouldn't argue with that. He'd spent hours learning the best way to give Davey his medications, how to tell when he wasn't feeling well, what to look for if he ever started going into heart rejection. But after saying goodbye three times and then having a short conversation with Ms. Duggar who assured him that Davey's voice was not scratchy sounding just tired from playing rodeo that day, he had ended the call feeling satisfied.

He noticed that the crowd had been clearing out as he'd been on the phone and Sarah was alone, lost in her own thoughts now.

"I guess we better leave before they shut the doors on us," he said as the wait staff started cleaning off their table. Then he added, "What about tomorrow after the forums we take in some of the sights? I've never been to Dallas."

He didn't want the evening to end while Sarah appeared so unhappy.

"I was thinking about going over to Fort Worth, it's only a half hour away. The weather is supposed to be nice and they have a beautiful park that's made up of water gardens. I went there with a group from school one day," she said, smiling now presumably from an old memory.

And if a walk in a park was what would keep that smile on her face, a walk in the park was what they would do.

"I think you'll like it and if we have time we could visit the stockyards. It's more of a tourist place now, but it does have a very colorful history."

"Then it's a date. I mean—" He stumbled over the words. "It's a plan."

Sarah was next to David as they walked to their rooms. For weeks, she'd wanted to know how David would feel about learning that the donation of Davey's heart could have come from her son, Cody, and even after their conversation tonight she had no idea how he would take the news. Would he be angry that she hadn't told him earlier? She knew that was a possibility that he could feel that she was being untruthful by holding back the information she had. She'd have to explain to him that it had taken time for her to come to terms with the possibility herself. If anyone would understand the mixed feelings she felt, he would. He'd admitted himself that he wasn't comfortable trying to approach the donor's family.

"Are you okay?" David asked her as they stopped at her door.

"I'm fine. It's been a long day," she said as she inserted her key card and opened the door to her room. "I'll see you at noon? Downstairs after the forums?"

"That sounds great," he said as he looked up and then down the hall. "I'll wait for you to lock the door."

"Okay, good night," she said, then shut the door and latched it.

It had been a long time since someone had worried about her safety, not that she didn't feel safe when Jack was around. The man had a shotgun that could take down any rattlesnake or intruder. And it wasn't as if she couldn't take care of herself—Jack wasn't the only one who knew how to shoot that shotgun. But it was kind of nice to have someone care about her.

David was that kind of man. He wouldn't be as good of a doctor as he was if he didn't care about his patients. And she had never seen a more caring father. It was only to be expected that he would care for his friends.

Just friends, she reminded herself. He had taken her hand while they'd left the dinner with the rest of the crowd. A crowd that had threatened to separate the two of them, and it had made her feel an excitement that she hadn't felt in years. There had been no one since Kolton whose touch had affected her the way David's touch did. There had been a few men that had asked her out over the last couple of years, but she'd never been tempted by any of them.

We're just friends...we can be only friends, she reminded herself again as she fell asleep.

CHAPTER SIX

THEY DECIDED TO hit the stockyards first as they both wanted to eat at a small barbeque shop there that Sarah had looked up online. They ate their sandwiches and toured the museum before heading outside to watch the daily cattle drive of longhorn steers.

"I love the longhorn steers. Aren't they pretty?" Sarah asked.

"They're awful big and those horns are massive, but I don't think pretty is the right thing to call something that could trample you to death in seconds," David said as he moved closer to hear over the noise of the animals as they were herded in front of them.

"Davey would love it here," she said, though she could see the doubt in his eyes.

"He'd love it, all right. I'd be chasing after him while he chased those steers down the road. He's taken a big interest in the rodeo since I started taking lessons."

"Jack once told me that Kolton was in love with the rodeo by the time he was three, so Davey's a little bit of a late starter." They moved off the main road and followed the walkway that let by the specialty shops. "Hey, I want to look in here for a belt buckle for Jack. It's his birthday next month."

As she paid for the oversized silver and golden buckle with the Texas flag displayed on it, she saw David pick up a small toy steer.

"Davey will love it," she said as he showed the toy to her. He quickly paid for it then rejoined her, both of them heading back out onto the walkway.

"He thinks that he's going to grow up and ride one of those bucking broncos like he sees the cowboys do on TV. I don't have the heart to tell him that it's not something that he'll ever be able to do," David said as he put the toy back into its bag.

"He'll change his mind a thousand times before he's grown," Sarah said, though she knew that there could be a lot of limitations on what Davey would be able to do when he got older.

"My brother's little girl wants to ride a bronco too and she's only four. His wife caught her out in the pasture trying to climb a cow the other day and almost had a heart attack," Sarah said.

They walked back through the shops then out to where the steer were corralled. She told David about being raised on a cattle ranch and then about her time barrel racing on the rodeo circuit. She found herself mentioning Kolton in a story of the days he was on their high school steer roping team. She had spoken so little of her deceased husband except when she and Jack were alone, but it seemed that the more she talked about him the easier it was becoming. Maybe her mother had been right. Maybe she did need to talk to someone, only for now the only person she wanted to talk to was David.

She felt the pressure of his hand against her lower back as they moved through the crowd and she buzzed with excitement as a shiver raced through her body. It was like it was so in tune with his that just the merest of touches was enough to weaken those walls she had put up against feeling anything more than friendship for him. She felt the temptation to move back into him so that she could feel what it would be like to be held in his arms. It wasn't until he'd moved his hand from her back that she felt her heart rate return to normal. Did he know he was doing this to her?

"Weren't your parents a little afraid that you'd get hurt riding that fast," he asked after Sarah explained how the sport of barrel racing was timed.

"Not really. I mean barrel racing is a lot safer than steer roping or bull riding. It was just part of our life," she said as they headed back through the cloud of dust that still hung in the air after the steers had gone through.

"Thanks for sharing that with me," David said as he started the car.

"I'm glad you enjoyed it," Sarah said as she buckled herself in. She was enjoying her time with David but she couldn't continue to be a coward. She had to tell him about Cody, about that night. She couldn't live with this between the two of them any longer.

"No, I mean you sharing your memories with me. I know you don't talk about Kolton very often. I appreciate that you trust me enough with those memories," David said, then reversed the car.

She felt the heat of embarrassment as it flushed through her body. If she trusted David like he believed she did she wouldn't be holding back from telling him about that night. She had to make things right between the two of them.

* * *

After the noise of the stockyard, she was relieved to see that the water gardens were as peaceful as she remembered.

It had been Kolton who had first been so amazed by the gardens when they had made the trip with their junior class to Fort Worth. He'd already been fascinated with building things and had made up his mind to major in architecture at Baylor University by then so it wasn't a surprise that the architecture of the fountains would interest him.

"Let's go this way," she said as they turned a corner and headed toward the meditation pool.

"I came here with my high school one year and fell in love with this part of the park," she said as she took his hand and led him down the path.

While the other kids had rushed off to the larger terraced falls where they could wade down the steps to the pool below, she'd found the private meditation pool surrounded by cypress trees as a respite after the noise of the bus crowded with her friends. It was there that she would tell David about her son. Their sons.

"It's beautiful, isn't it?" she asked as she led him to a spot where they could sit. The lights had come on across the park and the sun had begun to set as they had walked through the collection of fountains that covered part of the grounds.

"It is," David said as he sat next to her. "It's very peaceful."

She looked around the area to see that very few people were remaining now. Now the time had come, she didn't know where to start. She decided on the beginning when she'd first seen David in that waiting room over three years ago, or maybe more appropriate was to start with the ending of a young life that was taken too soon from this world.

Sarah turned toward David, noticing that instead of looking at the fountains he was staring at her.

"What's wrong?" she asked.

"There's nothing wrong," David said as he moved closer to her. "It's been a great day. There's only one problem."

"What problem?" Sarah asked. The only problem she was aware of was the fact that she was sitting talking nonsense with David when she should have been leveling with him.

"Sitting here surrounded by this beautiful park and earlier when we were at the stockyards, the only thing I've been able to think about is how much I'd like to kiss you," David said. While his voice contained a teasing note, there was no laughter in his eyes.

She tried to make her mind concentrate on what he was saying, but all she could think about was the deep longing she could see in eyes that now appeared more of a smoky gray then their usual mix of green. She knew that feeling. She had felt it ever since he had touched her earlier that day as he had laid his warm hand against her. And before, when his innocent touches at the stable had sparked a long-forgotten desire in her.

"I don't know if it's the magic of tonight or something more, but I won't cross that line if you don't want me to," David said as once more he rubbed the back of his neck.

Sarah couldn't believe what David was saying. Did he feel it too? This connection that seemed to flicker to life every time they touched. His touch had sent her hormones into overdrive today, but she had thought it was only her feeling that way. How was she supposed to keep ignoring the desire she felt whenever he was close now that he had admitted his attraction for her?

"It's okay, Sarah, if you're not interested in taking things between us any further," David said as he slid away from her.

Deep inside her a desire that had lain dormant protested against his withdrawal. She felt torn between what her body wanted and what her heart was telling her. She hadn't been kissed since the morning she had kissed her husband goodbye for the last time as she had left for work. Even now with her body driving her to say yes, she felt the fear of the unknown bearing down on her.

But it's only a kiss...one kiss. Would it be so bad to let yourself feel what it's like to be alive for just one moment?

"Yes," she said, the word coming out loud as it seemed to echo across the park. She cleared her throat and tried again. "Yes, I'd like you to kiss me."

She felt stupid as she knotted her hands together in her lap. Could she feel any more awkward? She'd shared kisses only with Kolton and she wasn't sure what it was that she was supposed to do right now. Then David moved in closer to her, closer than he had been earlier and everything suddenly felt okay. This was David, a man who she knew she could trust.

He hesitated a moment, then bent down

and brushed his lips across hers before pulling back from her. His eyes opened and suddenly her own body was lit with the same fire she saw reflected in David's eyes. The force of the desire that claimed her body had her wanting to take a step back, but the need that David had kindled with just one small kiss held her in place.

He pressed his lips against hers again, this time teasing until they parted for him. His tongue met hers and her breath caught. When his arms came up around her, she instinctively moved into them. She forgot the park, the water, the night sky that surrounded them now. There were only the two of them, their bodies straining to be closer. What had started as a simple kiss was quickly turning into much more.

Then she remembered why she'd brought him here.

Pulling away from him, she straightened her clothes. What had just happened? It had been a long time since she had been kissed, but even that couldn't explain the way that kiss had made her feel. She had come here to tell David of her memory of that night in the waiting room and about her donating Cody's organs and now instead, she had just complicated things even more. She couldn't let things continue like this—but, oh, how she would have liked that kiss to continue. She had to set things right between the two of them.

"I need to tell you something. Something that I should have told you a long time ago," she said, then cleared her throat. "It's about the first time we met, well that's where it starts, I guess."

"At the hospital?" David asked, his eyes searching hers.

"Yes, but no," she said, and then held her hand up a moment before he could speak. "Well, actually we didn't meet exactly. I'm doing this all wrong. Let me start again."

"Okay," he said. She watched as his hand started toward his neck, then following her eyes he lowered it back down to the bench.

"That day in the hospital when Dr. Benton introduced you wasn't the first time I had seen you." She forced her eyes away from his troubled ones. She was doing such a bad job of this.

"No?" he asked. "Where could you have seen me? At another conference?"

"No, it was at the hospital, just not that day. It was earlier. Over three years earlier. The night before Davey's transplant."

"I'm sorry. I don't really remember a lot of the people that night. Were you part of the team then? Dr. Benton told me you'd only been working with the cardiac group for a couple years," he said. She could see a trust in his eyes now that she was going to shatter.

"That's right. It wasn't till after I lost my family, after that night I saw you that I decided I wanted to change my focus to the transplant team."

"I don't understand," he said as he moved closer to her. She felt the heat of his body before he took her hand in his. The night was turning cool and she turned into him, finding comfort in his touch as he placed his other arm around her. Even through her nervousness she could feel that connection to him that had begun to form. He'd known she needed his touch even though he hadn't understood why.

She took a deep breath, and then let it out. A cleansing breath they had taught her in birthing classes and that was exactly what she needed. She needed to be cleansed from this secret she had been carrying around with her since he had come back into her life. There was something changing between the two of them, something that scared her as much as it fascinated her, but this had to be dealt with first. Suddenly she knew where to start the story that had changed all her life and maybe David's too.

"I was at work on the surgical hall of the hospital when I got the call from the emergency room that my husband had been in a car accident and they needed me to come as soon as possible. Of course I didn't believe them at first. No one wants to believe that something like that can happen to them. They'd taken Kolton to another hospital, a hospital closer to the accident, so I had a friend drive me. I knew it was bad. I'd given bad news to family members enough myself that I knew, but I didn't think he'd be gone. Not like that. He was so young and alive. And there he was lying so still on the stretcher." She wiped a tear that had streaked down her face. She'd never shared the whole story of that day with anyone, not even Jack.

"I didn't think about Cody, at least not at first. Kolton was to drop him off at day care that morning on his way to work. I'd assumed the accident had taken place afterward. And then a police officer came into the room and told me that my son had been taken to the children's hospital. The one I'd just left. I don't remember much after that. I think it was the police officer who drove me back, I'm not sure.

"The next thing I remember was seeing

Cody lying in the hospital crib. He was so quiet, so still. Just like Kolton. The doctors and nurses were great, but there wasn't a lot they could do. The car had been T-boned by someone who had tried to make the yellow light. I guess Kolton didn't see them when the light turned green. It was a useless accident that shouldn't have happened." She stopped and paused for a second trying to gather her thoughts. "And that's how I ended up in the hospital waiting room the night that I saw you there."

"You're the woman who almost passed out," he said, his voice a little shaky. Was it possible he had figured out where her story was going?

"Yes. I'm not surprised you didn't recognize me. I'd been at the hospital for three days by then and they'd just told me that Cody was brain-dead." Oh, God, it hurt to say those words. Even after all this time it physically hurt. Her stomach churned with the pain that griped her and she fought against the nausea.

"Sarah, stop. You don't need to put your-self through this," David said as he pulled her even closer till her back rested against his chest and both of his arms.

"No, I want to tell you. I need to tell you so that you'll know," she said as she willed her stomach to relax so she could continue.

"Like I said, I had just been told that Cody…was gone. I knew of course, but I didn't have to face the reality of it until the doctors had run all the tests. I'd held out for a miracle, but I didn't get one."

"Of course I knew the people from Organ Procurement would be notified by the staff and then they'd want to talk to me about donation and even if I didn't want to donate, the doctors were going to want to talk about the next step. I already knew the next step. They were going to talk about taking my son off life support. I did the only thing I could do. I ran and hid." It had been useless, but at the time it had seemed that it was the only thing she could do. Jack had been waiting for her in the trauma waiting room with her parents and she couldn't face them. She had needed some time alone, so she'd found the waiting room as far away from the trauma unit as she could.

"And that's when you saw me?" he said, his voice low and soft now.

Night had fallen as she'd been talking and the stars were starting to come out, adding their sparkle to the lights that reflected off the waterfall in front of them.

"Yes, you were talking with one of the transplant case managers. I shouldn't have stayed there listening, but I couldn't make myself face my family. Jack had already lost his son and now I had to tell him his grandson was gone too. I couldn't do it, not yet, so I stayed where I was and then I heard her talking to you about Davey's chance at a heart."

"She said that it was just a possibility, nothing for sure, just that there was a possible donor that they believed was the right blood type. I remember. It was the first good news I'd had in a long time," David said.

"It was the first piece of good news I had heard in days too. I remember feeling happy for just a few seconds as I thought of your child being saved. At least there was one family that wouldn't have to suffer the pain of losing a child. It wasn't until later that I started to think that maybe the two of us had become connected that night. That maybe I was in the right place at the right time as I considered what to do about my dying son while I thought of other children, like your son, that Cody could help save." She felt David tense against her. "Hearing about how much your son needed a donation helped me make my decision to donate my son's organs."

"What are you saying, Sarah? Do you think there's a possibility that Davey got Cody's heart?" David asked.

Running his hands through his hair

he moved away from Sarah. He needed to think about this more rationally. This whole conversation had taken a turn that he hadn't seen coming. One minute he had been sharing what had to be the best kiss of his life, then suddenly Sarah was talking about how she had been in the waiting room the night he had learned that there was still hope for his son.

If he'd known the story, the timing of the death of Sarah's family, maybe he would have put things together, but he hadn't. Not that he blamed Sarah for not talking about the death of her husband and son. She was certainly due the right to keep that to herself and he could see the pain it caused her to talk about that time in her life. But why hadn't she come to him with this information earlier?

"I don't know for sure, but I think that it's a possibility. We both know that by the time the neurologist told me about the brain death determination, Organ Procurement had already been involved in the background. The nurses that took care of Cody would have been required to call them when Cody had first come in unresponsive and ventilated," Sarah said.

"What was Cody's blood type?" David asked.

"O positive," she said shakily, then looked up at him. "Davey?"

"O positive," he said. Like he'd told Sarah earlier, he hadn't given Davey's donor family a lot of thought since those few months after the transplant. And he'd thought of them only abstractly. The idea of it being Sarah's family seemed surreal. "It's just a start, but there definitely is a chance, a good chance, that Cody could have been Davey's donor. I don't understand why you didn't tell me? Why wouldn't you have told me about this as soon as you remembered?" If it had involved his son, he had the right to know.

"At first I didn't want to make things awkward between us at work and I wasn't even sure that I wanted to know myself. Then, when I got to know you, I didn't want you to think that I was spending time with you and Davey just because of the possibility of the donation," Sarah said as she wrapped her arms around herself.

"Is it difficult? Seeing Davey? Knowing that Davey could have Cody's heart?" he asked. It had to be, didn't it? It was hard just asking the question.

"At first it was, at least until I got to know him better and I'd be lying if I said that the possibility that my son's donation could have made a difference in Davey's life didn't make me happy. He's a very special boy, just like my Cody. When I first saw Davey with Humphrey, I admit that it hurt a bit. Cody had only been two and a half when Jack and Kolton came home with that pony. Cody had loved him immediately and when I saw how taken with Humphrey Davey was, it shocked me that I felt a moment of resentment. But then I saw that smile on Davey's face and I knew that he loved that pony as much as Cody had."

"I'm glad you told me. Whether Davey was the recipient of Cody's heart or not, I'm glad you shared this with me, but you should have told me sooner."

It hadn't been an easy tale for her to tell, but he still felt as if he had been betrayed.

The park was deserted now and the walk back to David's car was quiet, the silence stretching between them. The laughter they had shared earlier that day had been replaced with too many emotions. He was torn between wanting to hold Sarah and tell her he understood why she hadn't told him and wanting to holler out, *Why didn't you trust me with this before?*

He knew neither of those reactions would help them work through this and no matter what, he knew that was what he wanted. That was what was important for them right now.

David's mind was full of more questions than answers as he walked Sarah to her hotel room. So much had happened over the last few hours. What would it mean to the two of them if Davey had received Sarah's son's heart? There was no way for that not to affect Sarah or her relationship to Davey. And what if it turned out that Cody's heart had been donated to someone else? Would that make a difference? No, he was sure it wouldn't. He'd seen how Sarah cared for the other children on the unit, showing them all the love and attention possible.

"So, what do you want to do?" Sarah asked as they stopped in front of her room.

Remembering the kiss that the two of them had just shared, there were a lot of things that came to mind with that question. None of which he thought Sarah was speaking of.

"Did you ever write a note to your donor?" she asked. "The privacy policy of organ procurement states that if a recipient and a donor both want to meet they will contact them."

"No, I'm afraid I didn't. I should have, I'd planned to..." he said.

"You were busy taking care of a sick child all by yourself. It's understandable that any family, especially a single parent, wouldn't have had the time for writing a note," Sarah interrupted as she turned to insert her key card into the slot. "Would you like to come in?"

David thought about all the reasons he shouldn't enter Sarah's hotel room, none of which seemed important right then. She stopped and turned to him, a look of concern shadowing her face.

"I don't mean to pressure you. I know this is a lot to take in," Sarah said as she opened her door.

"You've had weeks to think about this, Sarah. I've only had a few minutes," he said interrupting her. He would never feel anything but thankfulness for the family that had given his son a new heart, but it was going to take more than a few minutes for him to consider where the two of them went from here, especially if that family was Sarah's.

He watched as she slid her shoes off then walked over to the window where the lights of the city shone before her before turning and smiling at him. She had no idea what it did to him seeing her there, memories of their kiss still fresh, her dress still wrinkled from their embrace.

All that day he had thought of nothing but kissing Sarah, but he had never imagined just how wonderful sharing that one kiss with her could be. And now that he knew just how sweet those lips of hers tasted all he could think about was tasting her again. But this time he wanted to taste all of her, to feel every part of her against him, but he knew this wasn't the time for that. He needed to process everything Sarah had told him and he needed to come to terms with the fact that she hadn't been forthcoming with him. But while his mind might know that he needed to take a step back, unfortunately his libido did not seem to want to take the time that he felt they needed and he knew if he didn't leave right then, he was going to do something that both of them might regret.

"I have to go," he said as he turned away from her, not stopping even when he heard her call his name.

CHAPTER SEVEN

DAVID STARED OUT the window into the city below him. He didn't know how long he'd been standing there, but the road in front of the hotel was empty now. Looking out at the building across from him, he had watched the lights go out one at a time and now most of the building was dark. He glanced at his watch. A quarter past eleven. It had only been ten minutes since the last time he had looked.

He'd called and checked on Davey when he had first returned to his room and had found that his son had already gone to bed. Ms. Duggar had sounded half-asleep herself when she'd answered the phone and had seemed a bit put out when he had questioned her about Davey's medication. He knew he had a bit of a problem with

186 SARAH AND THE SINGLE DAD

control as far as Davey was concerned but he'd born all the responsibility in taking care of Davey since almost the day he had been born. Unlike him, Ms. Duggar had seen Davey only as the healthy little boy he was now. He knew that things could change quickly and Davey could be fighting for his life again.

Unlike most people, Sarah understood his concern for his son's routine and his need to check on his son often. The couple of times he had tried to date, the women had not been that understanding. Sarah had taken him and Davey into her home and her life just the way they were. Was it because of the possible tie Davey had to her son, Cody? He knew that she had worried about that, had been afraid that he would accuse her of such things, but Sarah wasn't like that. She was a genuinely good person. Maybe at first it might have been part of what drew her to him and his son, but he knew that she felt more for them now.

The fact that he'd walked away from her tonight was a miracle. He'd wanted her more than he'd ever wanted a woman before, including his ex-wife. There was something between the two of them that made him forget everything but her. He'd never felt this deep a need, this hot a desire or this chaos of emotions that would not let go of him.

Yet he'd walked away from her. And why? Because she had hurt his feelings by not being totally forthcoming with him? He couldn't deny that hurt, but he knew it hadn't been easy for her either. Whether or not it was Sarah who had donated Davey's new heart or another family, there was no way to explain to someone what that gift had meant to his son. And now instead of thanking Sarah for that selfless act, he was sitting here alone in his room brooding because he hadn't had the nerve to stay and see where tonight would lead the two of them. Yes, he did need to take the time to think about everything Sarah had told him, but what if this was the only night the two of them had to spend together? He had promised his son that they would live each day as if it was their last together, but here he sat spending his time worrying about things that were in the past. Was this how he wanted to spend his life?

He looked over at the bed where a staff member had turned down the covers for him. He had no desire to climb in that bed alone. He had no desire to spend the night alone at all. He thought about going back to Sarah's just to spend the time with her. Only he knew it wouldn't stop at talking. They'd only skimmed the surface of the attraction they felt for each other and it had left the two of them wanting more. Besides, she had probably already gone to sleep.

But what if she hadn't? What if she was suffering through this lonely night just as he was? Making a decision, he grabbed the key card off the entry table and headed out the hotel door before he could change his mind.

* * *

He tapped on Sarah's door quietly and waited. He would leave if she didn't answer the door in a minute or two. If she'd managed to fall asleep, he didn't want to interrupt her. But he heard the lock click and Sarah opened the door. She'd changed into a long sleep shirt, but her face showed no signs that she had been awakened.

"Is something wrong?" she asked as she moved aside for him to enter the room.

"No, nothing's wrong," he said. He looked through the door that led to the bedroom and saw the bed was undisturbed. Instead, he saw a pillow and blanket on the couch which looked out the window. Had she been spending the night watching the same lights go on and off as he had?

"Then…" she asked, looking at him expectantly.

"I couldn't sleep," he said as he motioned to the couch. "I take it you couldn't either?"

"No. But that doesn't explain why you

came back," said Sarah. She had invited him inside, but she still stood next to the door.

Had he made a mistake coming here? Maybe she had been glad he had left when he did and now here he was looking like a fool arriving on her doorstep in the middle of the night.

Not able to stand the distance between them any longer, he walked back over to her and pulled her up into his arms. "I'm sorry I had to leave."

"I'm just happy you're back. I'm sorry I didn't tell you everything at first," Sarah said as she rested her head on David's chest.

"What's wrong?" David asked as he held her tight in his arms.

"It changes things between us, you know," she said as she buried her head deeper into his chest.

Putting a hand under her chin he brought her eyes to his. "Sometimes change is good, Sarah, and sometimes it's something we can't avoid. If this isn't what you want…"

She answered him with a kiss, slow and hot that pulled against every bit of his control.

"Can you feel it, too?" she asked him, her eyes feverish, telling him she wanted this as much as he did. He didn't have to ask what she meant. There had always been something between the two of them since the first time they had met. Not that slow burn of desire that had been building over the last few weeks, but that connection they had felt immediately as their friendship had built into more. He didn't understand it, nor did he want to at that moment, but he couldn't deny it either.

"Yes, I can feel it," he said before bringing her lips to his.

Her hands roamed over his body and heat spread through his veins with every touch. He palmed her breast then answered her moan with his own. His hand slid lower, his palm cupping her sex as she pressed against him.

"I want more," she said, panting as she arched against his hand. "I want you."

David loved the way Sarah responded to him and there was nothing he wanted more than her right now, but he didn't want to make a mess of this.

"Are you sure, Sarah?" he asked, "I don't know where this is leading and I don't want you to look back on tonight with any regret. Right now we can go back to just being friends, but once we cross into that bedroom things will change between us."

"No matter what might happen between us later, I want to take that chance. I want to be brave for once. I'm tired of being afraid of taking chances. For just a little while I need to feel alive. I want you to make love to me, David."

Picking her up, he carried her into the bedroom and laid her on the bed. He watched as she pulled the long shirt over her head then crawled across the bed to help him with his own shirt. The sight of Sarah in nothing but a small pair of panties overwhelmed him, making his fingers clumsy as they tried to work the buttons on his shirt until Sarah brushed his hands away. Opening his shirt, she pressed a small kiss to his chest and then started on the button and zipper of his pants. Unable to wait, he took her breasts in his hands and caressed them. Her skin was so soft. Bending down he took one nipple in his mouth and sucked.

In one night he'd already become addicted to the taste of her, the perfect mix of Texas sugarcane and the spicy heat of a jalapeño. He heard a moan, but he wasn't sure if it had come from her or him. He switched nipples then released it when she pulled away from him as she tried to push his pants down.

Stepping out of his pants and briefs, he followed her onto the bed as she crawled backward to the top.

"I'm really glad you came back," she

said. She reached out and ran a fingertip down his chest to his lower abdomen and stopped at his erection.

"So am I," he said. A shudder ran through him as her hands encircled him. He bent back over her breasts and took a puckered nipple into his mouth as his hands worked off her panties. He was already addicted to the taste of her.

He parted the curls of her sex with one hand. He pushed a finger inside her and found her hot and wet. He ran his thumb over her core as she pushed against his hand. He heard the rustle of foil then tensed as Sarah rolled on the condom.

"I want you," she said as she raised her hips to him. "All of you."

He slid deep inside of her and caught her gasp with his mouth as he lowered his lips to hers. When he thought he couldn't take any more, she took him deeper still. Her moans filling the room as she drove him to give her more.

He tried to hold back, wanted to make

it last, but the heat of her was too much. She opened herself to him, taking each thrust until he felt her body clench and spasm around him. He let her body take the control he'd held tight and let himself follow her over the edge.

Sarah quietly closed the door to Lindsey's room so as not to disturb the sleeping girl. It seemed they were finally making some headway with the infection that had attacked her lungs. They'd managed to decrease her sedation to the point where she could respond to people in the room, but she was still sleepy the majority of the time.

"How is she?" David asked as he came up behind her startling her.

For a moment she was frozen remembering the day before that they had shared. They'd enjoyed a late breakfast in bed at the hotel that had quickly led to a languid few hours of love making that she wouldn't be forgetting any time soon. It had been a magical weekend, but they both had their reasons for not wanting anything more. They had enjoyed each other and that was all. But why then did her heart still race when he looked at her the way he was right now?

Sarah gave her head a small shake. What would David think if he realized where her mind had gone? "She's doing better. Have you heard anything about when they are planning to take her off the ECMO?"

"Dr. Benton spoke to the pulmonologist this morning and they're hoping it will only be a few more days," he said. "I made rounds last night before I left and I didn't see her mother. I've spoken with Dr. Benton about my concerns about her being able to take care of Lindsey after a heart transplant."

Sarah stopped and stared at him. No, Hannah hadn't been there all the time, but she'd explained to him before that Hannah had a job and had to split her time between the two places. Speaking with Dr. Benton could cause big problems for Hannah if the older doctor decided to take his concerns to the ethics committee or the social worker.

"Look, I know that it seems as if Hannah isn't here very much, but I have no doubt that she will be there for Lindsey after her transplant. She's been taking care of her daughter by herself for a long time now. I realize you don't know Hannah, but you need to give her a chance."

"I've just seen this before, Sarah. You see the best in everyone, but not everyone is willing to be there for their child when they need them," he said. "Right now the most important thing for Lindsey is to have someone to take care of her. I just don't see her mother doing that right now."

"You can't judge everybody by your ex-wife, David. You have to see that. Hannah will be there for Lindsey. I know she will," she said making sure her voice was too low for anyone else to overhear. She understood how hard it was for David to trust and maybe he saw something in Hannah that she didn't, but the young mother deserved for him to give her a chance.

"I hope you're right," he said before turning away from her.

Sarah knew this went deeper with him than just Hannah. But she needed to make him see that most parents were not like his wife. He had made a good life for himself and Davey and he needed to let the anger of his wife go. He deserved better than to continue being burdened by her betrayal.

Only as she'd stood there telling David that he needed to move on, she'd realized that she fought against moving on without Kolton and Cody every day.

It had been two days since he had spoken to Sarah except for when they were rounding on patients together and he was getting tired of it. Maybe he was being a little too hard on Lindsey's mom, he had seen her come in the hospital the night before as he was leaving and from the uniform she wore he could tell that she had come from work. But Sarah's insinuation that he was judging Hannah by the actions of his ex-wife were wrong. Weren't they? He would never purposely do that.

The two of them needed to get together and talk things out. The silence between the two of them was not good for their working relationship. Okay, he could be more honest with himself than that. The truth was he missed his conversations with Sarah. He missed the way her eyes would light up when she told a story about one of the horses on the ranch or how she'd listen to him describe a surgery in detail and never get bored.

And he'd missed the feel of her in his arms every night since the one they'd shared at the hotel. He missed his friend and his lover and he didn't like it one bit.

Making up his mind to set things right with Sarah, he left the doctors' workroom where he had been reviewing Lindsey's X-rays and went to look for her.

Spotting her at the end of the hallway he watched as she gowned up before entering the room. He looked down at the app on his phone and saw that the patient's room she had entered was a readmission that Dr. Benton has asked him to check on.

Noting the isolation sign on the door and remembering that he had seen that the little boy's wound cultures had come back positive for a resistant bacteria, he gowned and gloved as he had seen Sarah do earlier before entering the room.

Sarah looked up from where she sat beside the boy's parents as she went over the paperwork on a clipboard in front of her, while the eight-year-old boy lay bundled in a blanket sleeping.

"Hi, I'm Dr. Wright," David said as he hunched down beside the mother. "You might not remember me but I assisted Dr. Benton with Bailey's last surgery."

"Is Dr. Benton here?" the boy's mother asked as she looked up from the paperwork she was signing. "Sarah says that

Bailey is going to need to go back to surgery."

"Dr. Benton asked me to come see Bailey this morning, but he does plan on seeing him today."

"I'm glad you came in," Sarah said. "I was about to text Dr. Benton, but you might want to call him yourself. I don't think the doctor that transferred him back to us last night had looked at Bailey's latest lab work. He's showing signs of sepsis. Both his white count and his lactic acid are up."

"You don't see a lot of this in children but it happens. We need to get him back into surgery. I'll call Dr. Benton and see when we can get an operating room, but do you have a minute?" David said as he moved to the door to pull off the disposable gown.

"Sure, just give me a minute to talk with Bailey's parents. I've already discussed with them the possibility that he would need to go back to surgery," Sarah said.

David hung up after speaking with Dr. Benton to find Sarah exiting Bailey's room.

"Dr. Benton is on his way over from the office to talk with Bailey's parents, then we'll get him prepped for surgery," David said as they both headed toward the nurses' station.

"His mom says he hasn't had anything to eat since yesterday so that shouldn't be a problem," Sarah said. There was an awkwardness in their conversation that reminded him of the reason he had gone in search of her to begin with.

"I was wondering if you'd like to have dinner with me and Davey tonight," David said.

"Dinner? Tonight?" Sarah asked stopping in the hallway and looking up at him.

"It's spaghetti night and I know Davey would love to see you. I know it's a work night but I should be out of the operating room by five so it won't be a late night."

David caught himself about to rub at the

back of his neck then stopped. He had expected a simple yes or no from Sarah, it was just spaghetti after all, but by the look on her face she was taking the invitation more seriously.

"So, is this like a date?" Sarah asked looking up at him.

"A date?" He hadn't thought of it quite like that, but he guessed it could be considered a date. "Is it okay with you if it is a date? I mean we won't be alone, Davey will be there, but it could be considered as a date."

"What time?" Sarah said, though he could still see some hesitation which he could understand. Accepting that they were actually having an official date, with or without Davey as chaperone, was a step toward a change in their relationship that they might not be prepared for. The night they'd spent together had been more spontaneous where this would be an intentional agreement.

"How about six thirty? I'll text you the

address," he said as he went to his contacts on his phone.

"Sure, six thirty would be great," Sarah said as a nurse started toward them. "There's Bailey's nurse, I'll give her an update on him. Good luck with the surgery."

"Thanks," he said, then turned back to see the next patient on his list. He'd have to skip lunch to get finished before surgery if he hoped to make it out on time, but with the promise of spending time with Sarah and Davey tonight he knew it would be worth it.

Sarah looked around the kitchen and couldn't help but laugh. Among the dishes and vegetables laid out on the counter, two handsome young men, one considerably younger than the other, were busy working together as if they were chefs on the latest television cooking show.

"Do the two of you usually dress for dinner?" she asked as she took in Davey in his dress shirt and pants then turned to check out David as he stood chopping onions with his own dress shirt sleeves rolled up to his elbows.

"Davey insisted," David said as he looked up from the cutting board and gave her a smile. "According to him, this is how you dress when you have company over for dinner."

"It's when you have a girl over, Dad, and you're supposed to tell her how pretty she looks," Davey said in a loud theatrical whisper, then looked over at her with a mischievous smile.

"My dearest, Sarah, you look lovely tonight," David said with the same ridiculous theatrics as his son which sent Davey into a fit of giggles.

"Well, thank you, Dr. Wright," Sarah said, playing along with them. She was glad she'd changed into a nice dress after work though she was still dressed a lot more casually than David and Davey.

"Nice kitchen," Sarah said as she moved around to the other side of the large island.

"Thanks," David said as he raked the onions into a large pot. "I lucked out finding this place when I got accepted with Dr. Benton, especially since it came furnished."

"And I have the best room ever, wanna see it?" Davey asked as he jumped down from the stool and ran down the hall.

"I've got this," David indicated with a nod toward the stove where scents of garlic and onions were pouring out of the pot. "Would you like a glass of red wine?"

"That would be great. I'll be right back," she said as she followed the sound of footsteps to Davey's room.

The room was large with a window that overlooked a small manicured yard. With the exception of college she had never lived on a piece of land this small. She'd grown up with open pasture surrounding a large farmhouse and wasn't sure that she'd ever be able to get used to having neighbors so close that you could hang out the window and shake hands with them.

"Look what Daddy brought me back from that trip you went on," Davey said as he picked the toy steer off the ground where he had built a fence from plastic building blocks. "He said that I could go with you next time and see those steers with the big horns at the yards where they keep them."

Sarah felt a slight panic when she realized that she was being included in their family plans. She'd taken a big step agreeing to a date, she wasn't ready to start planning family vacations, if ever.

"We'll have to see if Sarah can come when we plan to go to the stockyards. She could have other plans," David said from the doorway where he held out a glass of wine to her. "Davey, go wash your hands."

"I love the big window," Sarah said as she took the glass of wine.

"His room is usually more of a mess, but he decided to clean it up before you got here. I'm sure if you look you'll find a thousand of those plastic blocks under his bed."

"Wow, flowers?" Sarah asked as they made their way back downstairs and into the kitchen where she now noticed a small table for four sat in a corner.

"Davey insisted that we had to have flowers on the table. Fortunately there were still a few azalea blooms left in the backyard."

"How did the surgery go?" she asked as she took a seat at the island and watched David toss the pasta with some olive oil.

"Good. The infection wasn't that deep, but he did have more blood loss than we expected," David said as Davey ran in the room and held his hands out for inspection. An alarm went off on David's watch and he looked over at his son with some unspoken message in the look.

"Okay," Davey said as the boy moved to a drawer in one of the cabinets and pulled out a medicine dispenser.

"Davey's been learning how to make sure his medications are on time," David said to Sarah. She could see that this wasn't the best part of the day for Davey, but she had to give it to David for sharing some of the responsibility with his son.

"That is great, Davey. Did you know that sometimes we have to give pills to the horses?" They ate while Sarah shared some of her best tricks to get the horses to take their medicine and Davey asked questions about how Pepper and Humphrey were doing since he hadn't been to see them the week before, something that he pointed out to David with emphasis. They'd just started to clear the table when another alarm sounded from David's watch.

"More medications?" she asked looking over at Davey.

"No, it's the hospital asking me to call urgently," David answered as he moved into the hall to make the call. By the time he returned she and Davey had loaded the dishwasher.

"What's up?" she asked as she dried her hands on the dishcloth.

"It's Bailey. He's bleeding and needs to go back to surgery. Dr. Benton's daughter is in labor so he's signed off to Dr. Sherwood who is asking for me to come in to assist since I assisted with the surgery today," David said. "Dr. Benton knows about Davey so it's not been a problem…"

"It's not a problem now. Go. Davey and I will be fine," she said. She could see his hesitation and understood that he was torn between his responsibility to help Bailey and his responsibilities with Davey. "It's okay. I'll take good care of him."

"Okay," David said before he rushed off down the hall, then returned seconds later. "He's already had his medicine and he took a shower before supper.

"His bedtime is in—" David looked down at his watch "—thirty minutes, though he'll try to stretch it for as long as you let him."

"Can't I stay up a little later tonight since we have company?" Davey pleaded with eyes so like his father's that she knew she would never have been able to deny his request.

"No. Bedtime is nonnegotiable tonight," David said before leaning down and giving his son a hug. "Be good for Sarah and this weekend instead of one movie I'll make it two. Deal?"

"Deal," Davey said with a smile.

"Thanks," David said to Sarah as she walked him to the door. "I'll be back as soon as I can."

"Just take care of Bailey. Davey and I will be fine," Sarah said before she shut the door.

"Now, Davey. What do you want to do for the next thirty minutes?"

"Can you help me with the book Daddy bought me about horses?"

"Sure, I can. Go get into your pajamas

and bring back the book," Sarah said as she headed for what looked like a comfortable spot in the family room.

Half an hour later, Sarah had answered every one of Davey's questions concerning how to tack a horse and the different names for each part of the saddle and bridle, watched him brush his teeth and given him a drink of water. She'd missed this ritual of putting a child to bed. She'd spent hours of her life reading bedtime stories to Cody and hearing him plead for "just one more" before she turned out the light. How she regretted all the times she'd told him, "No more stories tonight."

Closing her eyes she let her mind wander to her memories of her little boy all dressed up in his dinosaur pajamas that had been his favorite as he begged for just one more story.

David knelt down beside the large recliner that sat in his family room. He felt a bit like the bear that came home to find Goldilocks asleep in his bed, except his version of Goldilocks had dark brown waves instead of golden curls.

Leaning down he brushed a strand of hair back from Sarah's face. Sighing, she turned her face into his hand then opened her eyes. Dark chocolate eyes blinked open then closed again. He had a couple choices here. He could let her sleep where she was or he could carry her off to his bed, which would be his first choice except for the fact that his son was asleep in the room next to his.

"Give me a couple minutes," Sarah said as those beautiful eyes blinked open again. He watched as she performed a full-body stretch that had him wanting to crawl into his recliner with her.

"How is Bailey?" Sarah asked, yawning then sitting up in the chair.

"He's stabilized. They'd already had him in the OR by the time I got there," he said. "I appreciate you taking care of Davey. Did he give you any trouble?"

"No. He wasn't any trouble at all. I had no idea how bright he was. He showed me the book you got him on horses and he had a lot of good questions," she said as she tried to climb out of the deep chair. David pulled her up from the chair and steadied her. "Thanks. I didn't mean to fall asleep."

"And I didn't mean to be so late," he said as Sarah moved into his arms. The warmth of her body against his had him pulling her closer until their bodies aligned perfectly. The feel of her breast brushing against him had him wishing he had gone with his first choice of action when he'd first found her sleeping. They would have been snuggled in his bed together by now.

"Look, I owe you an apology. I checked on Lindsey before I left the hospital and you were right, Hannah was there with her. I spoke with the night nurses and they said she has been there every night since her daughter went on ECMO," David said as he let Sarah pull back from him.

"I'm sorry too. I certainly don't have the right to tell you that you need to move on from what you went through with your wife. If anyone should understand how hard that is then it should be me. I've spent the last three years trying to work through my own issues," Sarah said. "We both have some baggage and I shouldn't have told you that your time for working through it was up."

He pushed the hair back from her face. Did she realize that in some ways she did have the right? Or at least the power? He'd taken what she had said and given himself a long hard look and realized that she was right. That it was time to get rid of the bitterness that he had carried around with him for the last six years. When he'd stepped in to check on Lindsey and saw Hannah at her bedside he knew that he had let his bitterness toward another woman influence his opinion of a young mom he didn't even know.

"I'm glad you did. I do have some issues. Lisa leaving like she did was rough. I suddenly had a sick young son to take care of and I'm sure that there were people who didn't think I was going to be able to make it on my own with Davey. I should have given Hannah the same benefit of the doubt that I needed with Davey."

"Thank you for that," Sarah said as she leaned in and placed a kiss on his cheek.

"And thank you for staying with Davey," he said as they moved to the front door.

"It was my pleasure," she said as she stepped outside the door then hesitated. "You don't have to do everything alone. It's okay to let others help you. It's not a sign of weakness as much as an act of sharing."

He stood there watching her as she walked to her car and he let her words sink in. There were times when he felt that Sarah could see through him into his soul. It was that connection again. That wonderful connection that had him wanting more with Sarah then he'd ever wanted from another woman. A connection that if broken he didn't know if he would survive it.

CHAPTER EIGHT

"BUT WHY CAN'T I go too?" Davey asked for what had to be the fifteenth time since they had left the house. His son had been clingy all day. David had been afraid that Davey could be getting sick so he'd taken his temperature, but it had been normal. He was wondering if he should have just canceled the night he had planned with Sarah. Jack had certainly proved that he could handle his son, but Davey in the mood he was in right then was a different matter.

"Sarah said that Jack was really looking forward to spending some time with you. You wouldn't want to let him down, would you?" he asked as he parked the car in front of Sarah's house.

"No," Davey said with an impudence that he had never heard from his son.

"Davey, if you can't be polite we'll go home," said David. Turning around he saw the tears and Davey's quivering chin. He should have cancelled.

"I'm sorry. I'll be good. I promise," Davey said.

To David's relief, his son was back in his normal high spirits by the time he got him settled with Jack and Sarah had brought the horses up to the house.

"I packed some food. There's a nice spot just off the trail that's perfect for watching the sunset," Sarah said as she threw some type of bag across the back of her horse.

Why hadn't he thought of bringing some food? When he'd overheard one of the nurses talking about a sunset trail ride she'd taken with her family on the ranch, he'd thought that it would be a great idea. When he'd asked Sarah about taking the trail ride with him she'd made him clarify that he was asking her as a date, not as her student, which made him wonder what she had planned for the night.

He eyed Fancy, who was pretending to ignore him until he started to climb onto her back. From the haughty look she gave him, he knew that she was no more impressed by his mounting form now than she had been the first time he'd climbed on her.

"Ready?" Sarah asked him as she turned Sugar toward the end of the road that led past the house.

They took the orange clay dirt road for a few minutes then Sarah took a trail that led into a thick covering of trees.

"I don't know that I could have found that trail if you hadn't shown it to me," he said as they wound themselves through the thick woods.

"It's one of the more hidden trails," she said as she stopped at a spot where two trails shot off from the one they had taken. "We'll take this one on the left and it will take us back down the one on the right."

They rode silently, neither wanting to talk. The only sound was the horses' hooves on the trail. Sarah pointed occasionally to a squirrel in the underbrush searching for a nut that had survived the winter. The woods demanded a reverence that David would have compared to that of an old library. They saw several birds, cardinals and gray doves that were getting ready to roost in the trees and he knew that at some point he would have to bring Davey on the trail. The thought of his son had him worrying if he had done the right thing leaving him with Jack. He hoped that he was behaving for Sarah's father-in-law.

The path took a turn and he started to notice the trees thinning out. A few minutes later they stopped atop a hill overlooking a bright green valley of new grass. With the covering of trees he'd not been able to see the sky at all except for small patches where the tree tops had thinned out, but from this spot they had a clear view of the sun as it started its path below the skyline. Pinks and oranges blended with blues and violets.

"This is amazing," David said as he dismounted from Fancy. Sarah took the reins from him and walked back into the trees where he watched her tie the reins to a low hanging limb.

"Come on," she said, as she led him farther up the hill, stopping where the view was even better.

"Let me help," he said as she started to unpack the bag she had brought with her. He took the small blanket and laid it out, and then took a couple bottles of water from her. Sitting down on the blanket, he exchanged a bottle of water for the sandwich she handed him. They ate in silence as the sun slowly sank and the colors of the sky darkened.

"Look over there," Sarah said as she pointed to the dark sky behind her where the stars were starting to come out and a big full moon had begun to rise.

"It's beautiful," he said, then turned to her. "Almost as beautiful as you."

When Sarah turned back to him there was laughter in her eyes and he had no doubt that she wasn't taking his compliment seriously. He watched as she lay back on the blanket and looked at the sky.

Lying beside her, David reached for Sarah's hand as they stared at the darkening sky. He had never been to a more peaceful place. The falling night had brought a cool breeze that brushed over the two of them.

Letting go of Sarah's hand he rolled toward her. He fingered a lock of dark brown hair that had fanned out from Sarah's head, then bent to touch his lips to hers with the same reverence he had felt for the woods they'd traveled through. "Thank you for sharing this with me," he said.

Sarah looked up into David's face and tried to will him to kiss her again. He'd made her feel as precious and fragile as a newborn foal, but she wanted more. She released the breath she hadn't known she was holding then sucked in another one with a gasp as David's lips grazed her cheek then traveled behind her ear then down her neck as he rolled over her. Her hands reached for him as his mouth found the peak of her nipple through the thin denim shirt she wore.

"I've missed you," David said when he pulled away from her.

"You've seen me every day at work," she said, then let out a frustrated moan as he pulled away from her.

"I've seen my friend Sarah and my co-worker Sarah. I've missed my lover, Sarah," he said as he began unbuttoning her shirt and removing her bra. His hands were cool as they touched her warm breast and then he replaced his hand with his mouth and she wanted to scream to the sky with the pleasure. But she wanted more. Squirming against him, she reached between them for the zipper of his jeans. Her breath caught as his hand skimmed inside her jeans and panties. He circled her most sensitive spot then dipped inside her with long, deep strokes that sent her hurdling into a climax that caught her off guard, but it wasn't enough—she wanted more. She needed more.

"You have on too many clothes," she said as she tried again to undo the pants that were keeping her hands from him. She wanted to feel the hard length of him so she could guide him deep inside her. She wanted him to fill that empty place that ached for him. She wanted to feel him come deep inside her while her body squeezed every bit of pleasure from him. But she'd never get what she wanted, needed, if she couldn't get the clothes that were between them off.

David rolled away from her then wrestled off his boots then stood to take off his pants. For one second she caught sight of his heart-stopping naked form against the darkened sky as he covered himself with a condom. Then he was kneeling down in front of her as he worked her boots off and then her pants. She'd never felt so needy in her life. When he finally came back to her she lifted her hips up to meet him, her body unable to wait any longer.

As Sarah felt her body reach for their climax she understood what her body had known before she had herself. She'd needed David to fill not only her body but also her heart. It had been empty for so long. As they rode out their climax together she let go of all the pain inside her. She opened herself up to David and let him see the woman who had held back so much of herself for the last three years.

Her scream of triumph swept through the trees and seemed to echo over the valley. Tears filled her eyes but she didn't bother to brush them away. Whatever it was that the two of them shared right there in that moment was more than sex, more than intercourse. For the first time since the day she'd lost her family, she felt whole again.

They lay there together and stared up at the twinkling stars above them. They could have been the only two people in the world right then and that would have been all right with her.

"We have to go back," David said, though he made no move to stand.

"I know," she said as she turned toward him. "Thank you for tonight."

"It was my pleasure," he said as he turned so that they were facing each other.

She had never screamed during sex before and she would have thought she would feel embarrassed, but she didn't. Maybe she'd run out of feelings after purging so many from herself tonight.

She heard the buzz of a phone from the pile of clothes that lay scattered across the grass. "It's Jack," she said recognizing the ring tone as the one she had set up for him and hoping she hadn't worried him because they had been out longer than they had planned.

They both stood and started searching. She located her jeans and slid them on before she pulled her phone from the back pocket. It just didn't feel right talking to her father-in-law while she was undressed even if he was a couple miles of trail away and there was no way he could see her.

"Hey, Jack. What's up?" It took a minute for his words to cut through the pleasant haze that had formed in her brain. "Are you sure? Yes, we're headed back right now. We're on our way. It's okay. We'll find him."

She ended her call then looked up into David's eyes. She knew he had heard the conversation and had to have realized what had upset Jack, but she made herself say the words out loud. "Davey's disappeared."

David tried to fight down the panic that had gripped him as he had listened to Sarah on the phone with Jack.

Davey had to be safe. It wasn't like he was lost in the mall where someone could have stolen him. He had always loved playing hide-and-go-seek when he was younger. He had to just be playing with Jack. By the time they got back to Sarah's house, Jack would have found him.

Fortunately, Fancy seemed to pick up that there was an urgent need for them to return to the ranch. Following behind Sarah, she'd sped up to keep pace with Sugar, but with only the moon to light their path they were unable to travel very fast. Finally they reached the road.

"Hold on," Sarah hollered back at him as Sugar took off in a run. He had just enough time to grab the saddle horn before Fancy followed her. He hugged the horse with his thighs and bent low as he saw Sarah do. He could see the reflection of light in the dark night and knew that they had to be close to the house.

Finally they topped a small hill and he could see the house in front of them. It was lit as bright as an airport landing strip with flood lights shining from each corner of the house.

His horse came to a stop so fast that it almost sent him toppling off. They were both off their horses and running for the door when they saw Jack coming around from the backyard with a large flashlight in his hand.

"Humphrey's gone too," Jack said as they sprinted up to him. "I'm so sorry, David. I only left him for a minute. I can't imagine where he's gotten off to."

The older man's hands shook, sending the beam from the flashlight skittering across the yard. Sarah took the flashlight and handed it to David, then took both of Jack's hands in her own.

"Tell us what happened," she said, as she walked Jack up to the front porch and sat him down in the closest rocking chair.

Jack looked pale and David could see that the man was visibly shaken by Davey's disappearance, but right then they needed to be out looking for Davey. As if reading his mind Sarah turned back to him.

"We need to figure out where Davey might have gone," she said, then turned back to Jack. "Start from the beginning. What did the two of you do after David and I left?"

David tried not to fidget as he listened to Jack tell them about the supper of hot dogs and chips and then how Jack had taken Davey down to the big stables.

"We came back up to the house as soon as I finished locking the doors. I could tell that Davey didn't feel well, but all he complained of was his throat hurting. He was in the family room, I'd put on a movie for him, and I left him there while I went into the kitchen to get him a teaspoon of honey. I thought maybe it would soothe his throat a bit." Jack turned back toward him, his eyes full of pain. "I'm so sorry, David."

"It's not your fault, Jack," he said as he let his hand rest on the older man's shoulder. It wasn't this man's fault. He wasn't responsible for Davey's disappearance. If the blame rested anywhere it was on David. He'd known his son was acting out of character and that something had to be wrong, but he never would have thought Davey would run off from Jack.

"You said you locked the stables. Did Davey know that they were locked? Would he have gone back there to see one of the horses?" Sarah asked.

"I told him I was locking it up and he saw the keys I had," Jack said. "At first I thought he was just in the bathroom. When he didn't come back I checked the bathroom downstairs and then the one upstairs."

"We played a lot of hide-and-go-seek when he was younger. Did you check under the beds?" David said as his mind searched for any explanation for his son's disappearance.

"But that doesn't explain Humphrey being gone," Sarah reminded him. "Jack, you go back and clear the house. Maybe the two things don't have anything to do with each other. Either way we need to know for sure that Davey's not in the house. I'll check out the stable behind the house with David."

He followed Sarah around the back of the house then down a hill where a much smaller building stood. Like the house, the building's bright lights shone from each corner. He could tell Jack had been in a hurry to meet them as he had left the double doors to the building wide open.

"Davey," Sarah called out as they entered the building. Though smaller, this building was set up much like the bigger one with a short aisle running between stalls that faced each other and a larger room at the end where tools and horse tack hung.

"Davey, are you in here?" David called as he went from stall to stall to make sure his son wasn't lying alone in one of them hurt and unable to call for him. Several of the stalls were empty, their floors swept clean. An older horse eyed him warily as he climbed up the metal bars of the stall door and looked past him, but the only thing besides the horse in the stall was a bed of fresh hay.

"David," Sarah called to him. Jumping down for the gate he ran toward her with visions of his son lying bleeding on the ground flashing through his mind, but when he made it to her all he could see was Sarah staring at a spot on the stable wall.

"Humphrey's saddle is gone," she said as she turned to him.

"I don't understand," he said. "Davey doesn't know how to put the saddle on the pony."

Sarah face fell. "Remember the other night when he was asking me questions about the horse book you had bought him? We went all the way through on how to get a horse ready to ride and he already knew the name of most of the tack parts." She headed back to where the stall doors stood open. Inside the stall he saw a small two-step platform.

She turned toward him, her eyes wide with fear that hadn't been there when they had been talking to Jack, and then she pushed past him running out of the building. He found her at the edge of woods that ran behind the building.

"Davey," she called out into the dark trees, and then ran blindly into the woods. He followed her, calling out his son's name. And soon was unable to tell which way led back to the stable and house. If Davey had gotten lost so easily, how was he supposed to find him? How was Davey supposed to find him? He saw the light from the flashlight Sarah still held and used it as a guide back to her. What had he been thinking to leave his son alone?

Davey was a precocious little boy who was always pushing the boundaries. And now his son was lost in the dark because his father hadn't been there to keep him out of trouble.

"I thought I'd lost you too," Sarah said as she threw her arms around him and waited for him to pull her closer, to comfort her like she was trying to comfort him.

"It's my fault," David said, his eyes staring out into the dark woods behind her. "My son is lost out there because of me."

"You can't think that. He's just a little boy who's fascinated with horses who decided to go an adventure," she said as she once more tried to get David to look at her. "We'll find him."

"He wanted to go with us and I told him he couldn't. He was tired this afternoon and I should have kept him home, but I was looking forward to spending time with you. I should have kept him home, Sarah. I'm his father, I'm supposed to put him first," he said before he turned away from her and headed back toward the house.

CHAPTER NINE

As DAVID TOOK his car and headed back to the stable to look for Davey, Sarah sat Jack down and they went over the night again. She tried to not let the things David had said bother her. He was scared for his son and it was natural that he would blame himself, but it hadn't been his words that had hurt. It had been the way he'd pulled back from her. He'd shut her out with his actions more than his words.

She made herself concentrate on what was important right then. There would be time for her and David to talk later. Right now they needed to find Davey. She would have to call the police and ask for help, something she didn't want to do if the boy was just hiding nearby.

"The only thing that makes sense is

that Davey took Humphrey to go look for David," Jack said. "I just don't understand why that pony hasn't brought him home by now. Most of the time all he does is meander around in the yard. The only time he's ever been out of the backyard was…"

"You said that he should have come home," she said as she jumped up and looked for the keys to the ATV. "Remember where he went a couple months ago when someone left the gate open?"

"Yeah, he'd gone back to that little stable you and Kolton built," Jack said as he started to stand, realizing what Sarah had as well.

"Exactly. Stay here. I'll call you as soon as I get to the house. Tell David I know where Davey is."

Why hadn't she thought of this earlier? Kolton had built a two-stall stable after they had bought the pony for Cody. It was where they had kept Humphrey until Sarah had moved back in with Jack. It had been Humphrey's first home with them, it only made sense that he would head there if he was let out.

Sarah turned the key and hit the gas. The four-wheeler jumped to life, hit the corner of the front ditch in her urgency then righted itself as she turned it up the clay road. She remembered to turn the lights on after a close call with a tree-lined curve.

She left the ATV running with the lights on as she grabbed her flashlight and jumped out. She ran toward the house then stopped. She'd had the utilities turned off after a few months of living with Jack. The idea of walking back inside the house after losing her family had been too painful. Her momma and her brother's wife had packed up her clothes and a few other things that they felt she needed and Sarah had chosen to leave the rest of things where they had been that last day that Kolton and Cody had left the house. She stood staring at what was supposed to have been her forever house. She wanted to turn her back and walk away, but there was a little boy lost and she had to make sure that he wasn't here.

"Davey," she called as she walked up the driveway, then followed the sidewalk up to the front door. She checked it even though she knew she'd find it locked. "Davey, can you hear me?" she yelled as she headed to the back of the house where Humphrey's stall had been.

Davey, please be here.

The door to the tiny stable stood open and she pointed her flashlight inside. A large shadow moved startling a scream out of her that quickly became a laugh. Standing in the dark, was the pony giving her a very put-upon stare. "Davey, where are you? It's okay, you can come out."

Pushing past Humphrey, she searched the stall then ran around to the other stall. He wasn't there? That couldn't be right. Davey would surely have stayed with the pony. Unless he had fallen off. What if he had fallen off? What if he was lying out in the woods hurt? Would the pony have left him? She didn't think so, but she never would have thought that Davey would have taken off on the pony either.

She left Humphrey in his stall and re-traced her way back to the ATV.

"Davey," she hollered louder now. "Davey?"

She listened for an answer as she checked behind the overgrown hedges that lined the front of the house. As she passed one of the windows she thought she heard something. She checked both sides of the bushes, then heard a soft cough. It was coming from in-side the house. She ran back to the front door but it was locked just like the first time she had checked it. She sprinted to the back door.

"Davey?" she called as she turned the knob. The door opened easily. Using her flashlight she checked each room as she came to it, flashing the light into each cor-ner. Another cough came from the end of the hall. She entered the room for the first time since she'd lost Cody. Her light hit the blue curtains that hung over the window and then came to rest on the little boy curled up on a bed way too small for him. She bent down and picked the boy up and wrapped him in the animal-covered comforter.

"Davey, it's Sarah." She touched her hand to his forehead then checked his pulse. He was warm and his heart rate was a little fast which could be explained if he had a fever, and though his respirations were even they did seem a little labored. She carried him out to the four-wheeler and laid him on the seat, then pulled out her phone, her fingers trembling as she went through her contacts. She'd managed to hold the tears off until David answered and she heard the desperation in his voice.

"David, I've got him. I've got Davey," she cried through the tears.

David took his first deep breath since Sarah had received Jack's call telling them

Davey was missing. He'd been about to dial the emergency number after he hadn't found Davey anywhere around the stables when Sarah had called. He still didn't understand why his son would have gone off like that, but he did know that it wasn't something he would be taking a chance with ever again.

Pulling his car up to the house, he could see the lights of the ATV as it topped a hill on the road and he held his breath as he watched it headed toward him, then stop in front of the house.

"Hey, Daddy," his son said as Sarah lifted him off the bench of the vehicle and handed him to David. "I'm tired. Can we go home now?"

"Hey, buddy. Let me check you out first," David said as he hugged his little boy tight to him. There had been so many times in his son's life that he had thought he might lose him, but he had never imagined that he could lose his son like he had tonight.

"Let's get him inside. He's a little warm. I've got a thermometer in the house," Sarah said as she opened the door for them.

"We found him, Jack. Humphrey went back to the house, just like you said," David heard Sarah shout as she entered the house.

He followed her, then stopped when he saw the man that Sarah considered a second father sitting at the table looking tired and older than he had ever seen him.

"It's okay, Jack," Sarah said as she went to the man David knew she loved as much as she had loved his son. "Davey's okay."

Only David knew exactly how Jack felt, and he wasn't sure how easy it would be to get back to being okay.

David fixed the faded blanket decorated with cartoon animals so that it covered his son better as he watched Davey sleeping on the bed in the ER. He wondered exactly how many times he had sat in emergency rooms just like this one while he waited for Davey's lab tests and X-rays to come back. Ten? Twenty? More?

He should have been more in tune with what was going on with his son. He knew that Davey wasn't usually such a fussy child. He should have known that he was getting sick. He of all people knew how fast a small infection could turn into something worse where his son was concerned.

The night's growth of stubble scraped against his hand as he rubbed at his face, trying to remain awake. He'd spent many long nights sitting with Davey and even more on his rotations through his residency, and he'd still been able to function the next day, but the stress of the night was taking a toll on him. He jumped up as the door to Davey's room opened and the petite blond doctor that had seen Davey when he had first arrived came back into the room.

"You've got the X-ray back?" he asked before the women could speak.

"We did, and the labs too. If you want to go see them, we can walk back to my desk," she said.

David looked down at Davey. He wanted to see the labs and the X-ray film for himself but what if his son woke up while he was gone? Davey had been alone for hours in the woods; he couldn't leave Davey alone now.

"That's okay. I'll look at them later. What did the radiologist report say?" he asked. He couldn't remember the doctor's name though he was sure she'd introduced herself earlier.

"There is a small pleural effusion in the left lower lobe, but from the rest of the lab work I think Davey might have a slight case of pneumonia. I've sent all the results to Dr. Benton for a second opinion, but from the complaints that he had earlier that's my professional opinion. His white count is just above thirteen so I'll start him on some antibiotics. There's a nasty respiratory infection going around the schools right now. Whether exposure to that is the cause of Davey's infection or if it's his increased risk due to his transplant, I can't tell you. But I'm going to start him on an IV infusion and I'd like to admit him for observation at least for the next forty-eight hours just to be safe. Do you have any questions?"

"Not right now, but I would be interested in seeing his labs and of course I'll talk to Dr. Benton when he comes in this morning," David said. He didn't want the woman to think he didn't trust her opinion, but he was glad that she had consulted Dr. Benton.

"If you think of anything else you'd like to ask me or if there are any other tests you feel we should run just have the nurse let me know," she said before she left the room, shutting the door quietly behind her.

She'd done everything to put David at ease and more, but it was the fact that he hadn't listened to his intuition when he had first thought that his son was sick that still stuck with him. He'd known something was wrong when Davey had come home from school, but he ignored all the signs because he had wanted to keep his date with Sarah. What kind of father did that make him? He'd put his own desires ahead of his son's needs. That was exactly what Lisa had done. And he wouldn't make that mistake again. From now on Davey would be his only priority.

"It's going to be okay, Davey," he said as his son stirred under the covers. "I'm here. I'm not going to ever leave you again. I promise."

Sarah sat beside Jack in the hard plastic chairs that seemed to line every emergency waiting room. It had been almost two hours since Davey had been brought in. She'd hoped that David would be able to come out and update them, but her patience for waiting till he returned was wearing off.

"Maybe you should go back there and

check on them," Jack said from beside her. Her father-in-law had been quiet the whole trip to the hospital and had said only a handful of words since they had arrived.

"I will. Would you like a cup of coffee? I can raid the staff kitchen, they won't mind."

"That would be good," Jack said, then looked down where he had his cowboy hat in his lap. "If Davey's awake, I'd really like to see him."

"I'll be back in just a few minutes," she said as she patted his arm. She knew that Jack was feeling guilty that Davey had been lost while he'd been watching him, but no one could have expected that the boy would take off on an old rundown pony.

After finding a nurse that she recognized, she'd been able to get the information of which room had been assigned to Davey. Opening the door quietly, she saw David messing with the old blanket that covered Davey.

"Yours?" he asked as she shut the door behind her.

"It was Cody's," she said as she looked over the little boy lying on the stretcher between the two of them. Davey's cheeks had lost their bright red color telling her that the fever had broken and his respirations appeared less labored than they had when she had first found him.

"And the house where you found him, it was yours too?" he asked.

"Yes," she said. She'd tried to ignore the existence of that house, her and Kolton's forever home, but after walking through those rooms she knew that it was time for her to face the house and all the memories it held.

"Sarah," said a small voice from the stretcher. Davey's green eyes stared up at her with confusion. "I had a dream and you were in it."

"Hey, Davey," David said to his son. "How do you feel?"

"I'm okay," Davey answered as he

looked over at his dad, and then looked back at her. "It was you that I dreamed about. You and Humphrey, and you too Daddy."

"It wasn't a dream," she said, it had been more of a nightmare, but she didn't want to tell Davey that.

"You and Humphrey went on quite an adventure. Do you remember Sarah finding you?" David asked.

"Is it okay to go and get Jack?" she asked and was relieved when David nodded his agreement. She didn't think he held any hard feelings against Jack, but she knew there were some people that would have insisted on blaming him. But not David, he seemed to be insistent that it was his own fault instead.

When she returned, David had set the head of the bed up and was trying to get his son to take a sip from a straw. She felt the older man tense when the boy's eyes dropped down to the bed when he saw Jack come in beside her.

"Do you have something to say to Mr. Jack, Davey?" his father asked.

"I'm sorry, Mr. Jack. I know I shouldn't have gone off without telling you." Sarah saw the boy's eyes shoot to his father. "And I won't do it again."

"That's okay, Davey," her father-in-law said as he moved closer to the little boy's bed.

"Won't do what again?" David asked his son in a stern tone that left no room for the boy to scout around it.

"I won't go off without telling Mr. Jack," the boy looked over at his daddy. A silent message seemed to pass between the two of them. "And I won't go off on my own ever again until my daddy says I'm old enough."

"Why did you leave, Davey?" Jack asked.

"I just needed my daddy, but I promised him that I wouldn't do that again," Davey said, then yawned.

The speech seemed to have taken everything out of the boy as his eyes once more appeared heavy with sleep. The three adults stood and stared down at him until once more he seemed to have fallen back asleep.

She waited for David to ask her to stay with him, when Jack told her that he was going to head back to the farm, but he didn't. Still, she wasn't ready to leave the two of them yet so she made up an excuse to hang around the hospital a little longer.

"I think I'll get changed and go up on the unit and check on Lindsey and I might as well round on a couple of the new surgery patients too," she said. "Will you be okay driving back on your own?"

"I'll be fine," Jack said. "I've spent many a night waiting for a mare to drop a foal. I'll grab a cup of coffee to go."

She left the two men talking while she went and got Jack a cup of coffee to take with him, then told David that she would check back with him later.

After rounding on two new patients and writing an admission note for Dr. Benton, she went to see Lindsey. Entering the room, she was surprised to see Lindsey was not only awake, but the large ECMO cannulas that had taken the blood from her body and then returned it after oxygenation had been removed. While the little girl's color was still pale, some of the fluid that had been collecting in her body causing the swelling of her face and extremities had decreased, leaving her looking more like herself.

"Hey, Sarah," the little girl said with a small smile.

"Lindsey, I'm so happy to see you," she said as she went to sit down beside her on a chair that she'd last seen Hannah asleep in. "Where's your mother?"

"She had to go to work. I thought she might have been fired again—that's what usually happens when I get sick and she has to spend a lot of time here, but she says her new boss understands."

Sarah didn't know what to say. Had any of them really ever bothered to think about how hard it would be for Lindsey's mother to keep a job while having to go back and forth to the hospital on a regular basis?

She left Lindsey to get some rest and headed back to check on Davey only to find that he had already been moved to the pediatric acute care floor. Deciding that she would look in on him before she headed home, she looked up his room number.

"Hey," she said as she stuck her head in the door to Davey's room to find David standing beside his son's bed watching his son sleep.

"I used to do this all the time. Just sit there and watch him sleep wondering how long I would have him with me. He's been so healthy since the transplant that I've just taken it for granted that he would be okay.

"I dropped my guard, Sarah. I got caught up in my own life and forgot that keeping Davey safe has to be the most important thing in my life right now. It was my responsibility to keep Davey safe. Just mine. And instead of looking after him like I should have, I left him when I knew something was wrong."

Did he really believe that he was in this alone? Didn't he realize how much she cared about his son?

"I understand that you're upset. It's been a rough night, but you don't have to go through this by yourself. I love Davey. Jack loves Davey. We all want to be there to help you."

"Don't you see, Sarah. It's been me and Davey for years now and we've made it work. I'm sorry, it's just better that for right now I spend my time concentrating on Davey."

Sarah stood, staring at him. David hadn't explicitly said that whatever it was that they'd shared was over, but Sarah understood nonetheless.

She took a deep breath and chose her words carefully. "If you truly believe that, David, then I'm the one who's sorry. You can do everything in your power to keep the people you love safe and there are no guarantees in this life. Things happen. It's not anyone's fault, that's just the way life works." Then she held her head high as she turned and walked away, desperate to get out of the room.

She wouldn't let him see her cry. David had stood there and ripped out her heart and he hadn't even realized it.

For the first time since she'd lost Kolton and Cody she had let herself feel hope for a future and all it had gotten her was more pain. Just the possibility of a new family with David and Davey had made her feel alive and now she felt torn in two.

"What's wrong?" Jack asked as she came to sit by him at the table the next morning where he was reading the newspaper. "Is it Davey?"

"Davey's fine," she said, not wanting him to worry. "I'm just tired."

"And since when did your being tired

cause you to cry?" Jack asked. "Sometimes just sharing what's troubling you can be a help."

After the death of Kolton and Cody Sarah had spent hours talking to Jack. He'd been the only one to understand what she was going through because her loss had been his loss too.

Pouring herself a cup of coffee from the pot on the table, Sarah told Jack everything. He listened as she explained how she had first seen David that night at the hospital when they had lost Cody and the suspicions she had concerning the donation. She told him about the notes they had both sent to the organ procurement organization and how they were waiting for responses. She admitted to Jack that what she was feeling for David had become deeper than friendship, then ended with how David had pulled away from her because he didn't feel he could have a life himself and be there for Davey.

"Look, David's upset right now. He

might not be thinking straight because he's concerned about his son, but I've seen the way he looks at you. He cares for you, Sarah. It doesn't sound like he had much of a relationship with his first wife, not like you had with Kolton, so he doesn't understand the feelings he has for you. Tell me something," he said as he pushed back from the table. "What would you have done if Kolton had tried to push you away?"

"I'd have pushed back at him," Sarah said as she realized where her father-in-law was going with the conversation.

"It seems David's first wife ran at the first sign of trouble. Maybe that's what he's afraid of. Maybe he just needs someone to push back at him instead of running away," Jack said before getting up from the table. "What do you tell your students when they fall off a horse?"

"I tell them to get back up there. You can't let one fall stop you," she said as she smiled for the first time that day.

"Then it's time for you to get back on that horse," Jack said with a smile before he headed out the back door leaving her to consider his advice.

CHAPTER TEN

THE PHONE BESIDE Sarah's bed was ringing. She could hear it, knew that she needed to answer it, but she couldn't seem to find it. She turned over and felt the hard case under her left hip.

"Hello," she said as she hit the button on her phone. Looking outside she realized it was still dark. Had something happened to Davey? Suddenly awake, she grasped the phone and checked the caller ID. It was the hospital. "Hello? David?"

"Sarah? It's Betsy, from the cardiac unit. I'm sorry to wake you, but Dr. Benton said you'd want to know."

"Know what, Betsy? Is something wrong with Davey?" she asked as she jumped out of bed. She was sure she had left a pair of work pants lying out on her bedroom chair.

"I'm sorry, I don't know anything about Davey," the unit coordinator said.

Sarah sat down hard on the chair that she'd been balancing against as she tried to coordinate her legs enough to get them into her pants. "Betsy, it's—" she looked over at the clock by her bed "—four o'clock in the morning—can you please tell me why Dr. Benton wanted me called?"

"Oh, yeah, it's Lindsey. He wanted you to know that they have a heart for her," Betsy said.

"Hang on, just a sec," Sarah said.

She finished pulling on her pants, and then started looking through her closet for a shirt.

"Are you still there?" Betsy asked her as she came back on the phone. "The charge nurse wants to talk to you."

"Sarah, it's Tammy. Sorry about all this confusion, but Dr. Benton said that you could help."

"Of course, what do you need?" She'd

be glad to help if someone would just explain to her what was going on.

"It's Hannah. We can't get her on the phone," the charge nurse said. "We're going to get Lindsey ready, but we really need to get her mother here."

Sarah found a pen and wrote down an address. It wasn't far from the hospital, but it wasn't a neighborhood that she was familiar with. "I'm headed out now. Tell Dr. Benton that I'll have her there." She just hoped that it was a promise she could keep.

An hour later, Sarah drove into a small group of apartments that had seen better days, though it was doubtful that they had ever been much to look at. Checking the house number on the piece of paper, she knocked on the door and waited. A startled Hannah came to the door and soon Sarah had her dressed and on the way to the hospital.

"I'm sorry. I worked closing last night, and then I had to study." Hannah said.

"What are you studying for?" Sarah asked, though she had seen the books lying out on the small table in the small living room.

"I'm taking nursing courses," the young woman said, then looked away. "You probably think I'm wasting my time."

"I think that is great. Does Lindsey know?" Sarah asked.

"Yeah, but I didn't want her to say anything," Hannah said.

Sarah pulled into the parking place and turned toward her. "Lindsey loves you and I know she's proud of you. I'm proud of you too. This transplant will change both of your lives and if I can help, I will. I mean that, okay?"

Sarah was beginning to realize that Hannah had been too proud to ask for help or maybe she hadn't felt that she could ask for help. As Sarah watched her head down the hallway at a run toward her daughter's room, she thought of the other person she needed to see that didn't want to accept help.

David jerked awake. He hadn't meant to fall asleep—he'd just been going to rest his eyes for a moment. He looked down at his watch and saw that he'd slept most of the night. Stretching, he stood to check on Davey who seemed to be sleeping comfortably, and was shocked to find Sarah asleep in the chair across from him. He'd assumed that she had gone home hours earlier. After checking Davey's forehead and pulse, he moved over to Sarah.

"Sarah," he said as he squatted by her chair. He watched as her eyes blinked open then widened when she saw him. "What are you doing here?"

"Oh, I'm sorry. I didn't mean to fall asleep," she said, then gasped, "What time is it?"

"It's early. Why?" he asked, then moved away from her, away from the temptation to take her in his arms. He needed to keep her at arm's length until he could learn to control himself better around her.

His life had never been a peaceful one. It had been messy and stressful with an ex-wife that had cared more for her career than for their child who needed a lot of medical attention and care. He had accepted that this would be his life after Davey had been born and Lisa had left. And as Davey had lain there in his crib, not knowing that his mother had walked out on them, he had promised his son that he would always be there for him, that he would make whatever sacrifice he needed to take care of him. Turning away Sarah had to be the hardest sacrifice he had ever made.

"Did Dr. Benton call you?" Sarah asked as she moved over to where he stood beside Davey's bed. "About Lindsey?"

The little girl's name brought him back to whatever it was that Sarah was saying.

"What about Lindsey? Did she have a

relapse?" he asked. The girl had seemed to be improving when he had last seen her. Had that been two days ago or had it been three days? The days were all starting to run together now.

"No, it's a heart, David. They have a heart for Lindsey," Sarah said as she grabbed both his forearms with her hands.

"That's wonderful. I know Dr. Benton had his doubts that she'd get a transplant in time, but that doesn't explain why you're here."

"I thought you might want to assist the transplant team and I knew you'd feel better about it if there was someone to stay with Davey for you," she said as Dr. Benton opened the door.

"I hope I'm not interrupting, but we've got an ETA from Dr. Dreaden and Anesthesia is about to take Lindsey back to the OR," Dr. Benton said.

David looked from the doctor to Sarah.

"I'll be right there," he said, then waited till the doctor had closed the door.

"I'll take care of him, David. Go help with the surgery. You know you want to. We'll both be waiting for you when you get back," Sarah said before taking a seat next to his son's bed.

He couldn't understand what was going on. He thought he had made it clear to Sarah that he couldn't allow himself to make another mistake like he had the night before, but here she was offering to help him once more.

"We'll talk when I get back," she said.

Moving to where Davey slept, David ran his hand through the boy's curls.

He knew he needed to go change into his hospital scrubs, but he couldn't seem to pull himself away from his son. He'd been so scared when Davey had been lost. He had almost lost the boy twice before he had received a transplant and the helplessness he had felt then had been paralyzing. The possibility that he could have to face that again was very real and he had no control over that, but to lose his son because he hadn't been there when his son had needed him was unforgiveable and he wouldn't let that happen again.

"If he wakes up, tell him I'll be back as soon as I can," he said, then left the room.

Sarah sank into the chair David had occupied earlier. This had sounded much easier while she had been talking to Jack, but coming here and putting her heart back on the line again while she waited for David, while she acted like everything was fine, was the scariest thing she had ever done.

"Sarah," Davey called from the bed. "Where's my daddy?"

Sarah leaned over the bed and smiled down at Davey. David wasn't the only one who had been scared the night the little boy had wandered off and gotten lost. "He had to go help a sick little girl. But he told me to tell you that he would be back as soon as he could. Until then you're stuck with me."

"That's okay. Is my daddy helping the little girl get a new heart like the doctor helped me?" he asked as he sat up in bed. "He says it's very important that you get exactly the right heart."

"It is important and that's exactly what he's doing. Now what do you feel like eating this morning? I have it on good authority that the pancakes are the best thing on the menu," she said as she hit the nurse call button so that she could let the nurse know that Davey was awake.

"Pancakes are my favorite," he said.

"They're my favorite too," she said. "Now the two of us are going to have a long talk about taking horses without permission."

"Am I in big trouble?" he asked. She wanted to tell him no. She had been so happy when she found him that she would have forgiven him for anything, but things could have turned out differently. Davey had to learn that wandering off at any time without letting an adult know where he was going was not acceptable.

"It's not that you're in trouble, it's that you put yourself in danger and you scared me and your daddy."

By the time his pancakes had arrived, they had gone over all the rules of not taking off without telling an adult and not taking an animal that he didn't have permission to take. And he had told her all about his adventure with Humphrey when he'd gone out to find his daddy. An adventure that had caused him to tire.

"And then I saw this big house, but there wasn't anybody there," Davey said, then yawned. "I don't know where all the people were. Do you?"

"I'm afraid there hasn't been anyone living in that house for a long time," she said.

"Why not?" he asked. Sarah watched as his eyes began to close.

"Let's leave that story for another day," she said, and wondered if after the way she and David had left things if there would be another day?

The door opened and she recognized one of the case managers with the organ procurement program as she slipped into the room.

"I don't want to disturb you, but the unit coordinator on the floor told me I could find you here," she said as she looked over at Davey with more than a little curiosity.

"Did you hear that they received a heart for Lindsey?" Sarah asked her.

"I did and I checked on her mother. She's holding up," the woman said.

"The secretary at the office heard I was coming by and asked me to drop this off," she said as she held out a small envelope.

Sarah stared at the envelope. Except for her discussion with Jack, she hadn't thought about the notes she had mailed out to Cody's organ recipients in days.

She took the envelope and thanked the woman then stared at it after the door shut. She didn't recognize the writing on the outside, but that didn't mean anything. She'd decided to mail notes to all the recipients so that didn't mean that this one came from Cody's heart recipient. It could have come from any of the other recipients. There was only one way to find out.

David walked through the waiting room door with Dr. Benton at his side, exhausted but happy. It had been a difficult operation but successful and he was glad that he had been there.

Looking around the waiting room at the families grouped together throughout the room, it took only a minute to pick out Lindsey's mom sitting by herself. He knew that Sarah would usually have made time to sit with her if she hadn't offered to sit with Davey.

"Lindsey?" Hannah said as she walked toward them.

"She's fine," Dr. Benton said, then went

on to tell the child's joyful mother what she could expect over the next few hours.

Leaving them to talk, David excused himself and headed to check on his own son.

Sarah stood as soon as he opened the door. He saw the empty breakfast tray across the room and then his son sleeping soundly and he relaxed. Davey was a picky eater when he was sick, but by the empty tray it looked like he was feeling better.

"Lindsey?" Sarah asked.

"She's in recovery," he said, then looked down at the paper she was clutching in her hand. Were those tears in her eyes?

"Are you okay?" he asked as he moved closer, then stopped when she moved back from him. "What's wrong?"

"I received a note from Davey's heart recipient," she said, then wiped at her eyes.

"It wasn't the one I sent?" he said. Knowing that a part of her had been hoping that it had been.

"No, his name is Joshua and he has blue eyes," Sarah said, then sobbed again. Looking around for the standard cardboard box of tissues that was expected in a hospital room, he found one sitting beside Davey's bed.

"Why are you crying?" asked Davey from the bed. "Did Daddy hurt your feelings?"

"No, your daddy didn't do anything, sweetheart. I just got some news is all," Sarah said as she walked over to where his son lay. He was hit by the perfect picture they made together. With their dark heads bent together the two of them could pass as mother and son.

"I'm sorry you got some sad news," Davey said, as he looked up at her.

"It's not sad news," Sarah told him, "It's just not what I was expecting. It was actually a nice note from a very nice lady. And now that your daddy is back I'm going to run and check on some of the other patients on the floor while you tell your daddy about all the rules of taking a horse we discussed earlier."

David watched as Sarah slipped out of the door before he could think of anything to say to get her to stay.

"Are you sure you didn't do anything to make Sarah cry?" his son asked.

He started to deny that he had said anything that could have hurt her feelings, but he couldn't. He'd told her in the most painful way that he didn't have a place in his life for her because he had to put Davey first. He'd expected her to accept that things were just too complicated in his life for her. To understand that life with him and Davey would always be complicated. He'd thought she'd leave and not look back, but instead she'd shown up here today and entertained his son so that he could attend a surgery that she knew he'd want to be part of. Sarah was like no other woman he had met and yet he had sent her away. What kind of fool did that make him?

"I don't know, Davey, but if I did I promise I'll apologize," he told his son, then decided it would be best to change the subject. "Tell me what you were doing while I was gone."

"Sarah told me that what I did when I took Humphrey and left without telling Mr. Jack was wrong and that if I ever do anything like that again I won't get to ride any of the horses," Davey said.

"She's right. What you did was wrong," David said as he took a seat beside his son's bed. "You had a lot of people worried about you."

"I think Sarah would be a very good mother. She used to have a little boy, Mr. Jack said, but he had to go to heaven."

"I'm sure Sarah would be a good mother," David said.

"Good, 'cause I think it would be a good thing if you got me a mother," Davey said, then reached for the remote that operated the television.

David didn't know what to say to Davey's announcement. Davey had never said anything before about a mother and he had always assumed that he had accepted that it would always be just him and his father, but apparently he had been wrong. He had more than just himself to think about. Even right then he was being torn between wanting to go check on Sarah and wanting to stay with Davey.

He'd promised his son that he would always take care of him.

And you also promised your son that the two of you would live every day you were given to the fullest. But instead of going out there and doing what you want, you're sitting here, hiding behind your son and living a life of solitude.

Was that what he was doing? Using the excuse of his son needing him to keep himself from getting hurt again like he had been hurt by Lisa? Sarah had been right about living a life alone. That wasn't what he really wanted. He'd been so set on taking care of Davey that he'd isolated the two of them. It wasn't until he had come here and met Sarah that he had opened himself up to anyone else. He had to decide whether he wanted to isolate him and Davey for the rest of their lives or if he wanted to take that leap of faith and learn to trust others. One thing for sure, he wanted Sarah. His heart hadn't been the same since she had walked away from him the day before and he needed to put away his pride and admit that he needed her.

Picking up the phone, he reached out and asked for help, something that earlier that day he'd have sworn he would never do.

David had looked everywhere for Sarah. He'd checked Lindsey's room, but saw only Hannah at her daughter's bedside. Next he'd checked with the other nurses but no one seemed to have seen her. Then it hit him. He remembered when she had told him about the night she'd received the news that her son wasn't going to survive

his injuries she'd hid in the pediatric waiting room.

He saw her sitting in a small hidden corner. The sun had set and most of the hospital visitors had left for the day. He tried
to remember the night he had sat here,
where one of the case managers had found
him and given him the news that there
was hope for his son. He looked around
the room till he found a chair just a few
feet from where Sarah sat. Had it been
that one?

She didn't look up when he came to sit
next to her. He tried to think of what to
say, but he couldn't find the words. And
then he saw the note that she had held earlier, she still had it in her hands.

"This is the note you should have received," he said as he took the chair beside her. He held out a piece of paper of
his own, a note that he'd written her.

"I've already received a note. It's from
a nice family. They sent a picture. He's a
beautiful little boy. He has blue eyes like

Cody's," Sarah said as she stared down at the paper in his hand.

"But this is the one I should have sent you," he said as he tried to get her to take the note from him.

"It's okay, David. I was mistaken about Davey and even though you might not believe it, it doesn't matter. I still love Davey just as much as I did before I received this note," she said.

"I do believe you, Sarah. Look, how about I read this to you?" he said. What if she thought that what he had written was stupid? Why couldn't he find the right words to tell her how he felt?

"Okay," she said as she moved back away from him.

He cleared his throat. "Dear Sarah, I wanted to tell you thank you for the gift of love that you've shared with me and Davey…"

"But I didn't, David…" she started to say.

"Just wait and hear me out, okay?" he

said, then started to read again. "You've shown me a future that I've been too afraid to dream of until now. I hope you'll accept my love in return for yours and agree to a future together with me and Davey. Love, David."

He turned toward her and looked Sarah in the face. He had to face his fear of rejection head on now. But it wasn't rejection he saw in Sarah's eyes before she threw her arms around him and burst out in tears. He knew there were years ahead for them where there would be more tears, some of joy and some from pain, but as long they shared them with each other he knew they would be okay.

EPILOGUE

"PUT HER IN HERE," Davey said as he led the way through the house to his new little sister's room.

Secretly, Sarah had been afraid that bringing Kaitlyn into the same house that she had brought Cody almost seven years earlier would be painful, but instead it had felt right to bring his sister into the same room that had once been her brother's nursery.

After David had accepted a permanent position at the hospital, there had been the decision of where the three of them should live. While she knew they couldn't all move in with Jack, she couldn't bring herself to leave her father-in-law by himself. Her old house had been left empty for so long that there had been a lot of work necessary to get it livable and then there had been changes that both she and David had wanted to make, but when the renovations had been finished and Davey had moved Humphrey to the small stable behind the house they'd all agreed that they had made the right decision to keep the house.

She'd let her memories of Kolton and Cody be clouded by the pain that she had felt when she had lost them, instead of enjoying all the memories they had made together before that tragic day. Since moving back into the house, she had learned to share those good memories with David and Davey, which made her feel even closer to the family that she had lost.

Laying their new daughter in her crib, Sarah and David watched as Davey made faces at his little sister.

"Are you sure she's okay? Her face doesn't look right," Davey said.

He had worried about his sister since the moment they had told him that they were expecting, asking questions about whether she would have to get a new heart like he had. David had been very patient with him and they'd taken him to every obstetric appointment when they were planning to do ultrasounds so that he could see the pictures of his sister as she grew. Sarah herself hadn't worried about the baby as she figured Davey and his daddy were worrying enough for all three of them.

"She's perfect," David said as he stared down at his daughter.

And, surrounded by her new family, Sarah knew things really were perfect.

* * * * *

LET'S TALK
Romance

For exclusive extracts, competitions
and special offers, find us online:

 facebook.com/millsandboon

 @millsandboonuk

 @millsandboon

Or get in touch on 0844 844 1351*

For all the latest titles coming soon,
visit millsandboon.co.uk/nextmonth